Hello!

Whether you have a pet, hope for one, or dream of becoming a vet volunteer—or a vet!—I know that you love animals.

So do I.

I've had many pets—dogs, cats, mice, even salamanders. My best dog was a German shepherd named Canute. I got him from a shelter when he was two years old, and he was my constant running companion. He helped me get in shape for a half-marathon. A few summers ago, he died in my arms. I keep his collar in my office for inspiration while I'm writing.

The volunteers at Dr. Mac's Place love animals, too. I hope you enjoy reading *Fight for Life* as much as I enjoyed writing it.

Laurie Halse Anderson

The Vet Volunteer Books

FIGHT FOR LIFE

LAURIE HALSE ANDERSON

SCHOLASTIC INC.

New York   Toronto   London   Auckland   Sydney
Mexico City   New Delhi   Hong Kong   Buenos Aires

ACKNOWLEDGMENTS

Thanks to Kimberly Michels, D.V.M., and
Judith Tamas, D.V.M., for their consultation and
review of veterinary procedures and practices.

ISBN-13: 978-0-545-04464-6
ISBN-10: 0-545-04464-2

12 11 10 9 8 7 6 5 4   8 9 10 11 12 13/0

Printed in the U.S.A.   40

This edition first printing, January 2008

To my daughters, Meredith and Stephanie.
Thanks for your patience, encouragement, and
good jokes. May you always be wild at heart.

Chapter One

. . . .

"Mitzy, sit!"

Mitzy looks up at me and tilts her head to one side. She wags her tail, but she won't sit.

"Grrr," I growl. Mitzy whimpers and lowers her tail.

"Sorry, girl." I kneel and give her a hug. "I didn't mean to scare you. I'm just frustrated. Teaching you to sit shouldn't be this hard."

Mitzy is a full-grown Airedale terrier. Her short, wiry coat is mostly tan, with a big black patch over her back. She has a long nose, a stubby tail, small ears, and a confused look in her eyes.

The confused look is unusual for an Airedale. Airedales are usually very smart dogs.

"OK, let's try again. Pay attention." I stand in front of her. "Mitzy, sit."

Mitzy chases her tail and barks. This is impossible.

When Mitzy's owners brought her in, they warned me that she was a little "slow." I promised them I could teach her the basic commands. "There is no such thing as a dumb dog," I said. My grandmother, Dr. J.J. MacKenzie, taught me that.

Gran owns an animal clinic, Dr. Mac's Place. She says that all animals—even pets like cats, dogs, and guinea pigs—are wild at heart. Kids, too. I taught her that.

My parents died when I was a baby, and Gran took me in. I don't remember them, but Gran tells me I have my father's freckles and my mom's temper. Gran says taking care of animals prepared her for having me around. Very funny.

Some kids at school think I'm the luckiest person in the world, living with all these animals. It is fun, I have to admit that. Gran lets me help out with her patients at the clinic, and I sometimes get jobs, like training Mitzy.

Mitzy stops chasing her tail. I bet she's dizzy.

"Come on, now. We're not here to play. Mitzy, sit."

Mitzy takes a step backward. "Rouff!" she barks.

I pull up gently on her leash and use my other hand to push down her rear end. Once her tail hits the ground, she lies down and rolls on her back, begging me to rub her stomach. She thinks this is a game. If I rub her tummy, she'll think she can do whatever she wants in a training session.

"Come on, girl, stand up."

Mitzy rolls back over and stands up, giving herself a good shake.

"Mitzy, sit." I push down her rump. She stays in a sitting position for half a second.

"Good girl!" I shout. I scratch between her ears and hug her. The best way to train dogs is to praise them for what they do right. "That's enough for one day." I unclip the leash from Mitzy's collar and she takes off, running as fast as she can around the fenced yard.

Mitzy is nothing like Sherlock Holmes, my old, slightly overweight basset hound who's lazing in the shade by the oak tree right now. He's my only pet. But our house is attached to Gran's clinic, so I get to spend as much time as I want around dogs, cats, rabbits, hamsters, mice, lizards, snakes, birds, and the occasional horse or goat.

"Maggie!" Gran calls out the back door. "You have homework to do. Let's go."

Ugh. Homework. What a horrible word. It gives me the shivers. Don't get me wrong, I can do lots of things: I can shoot a three-point shot (sometimes), scrub the skunk smell out of dog fur, and even catch escaped guinea pigs. But homework? School? No thank you.

It's not that I don't try. I've been trying forever, it seems. But I always mess up. Gran has been getting serious about my grades. She keeps bugging me about asking for help when I get stuck and giving me the old "You're almost in middle school" lecture. When that doesn't work, she trots out the "You need good grades to get into veterinary school" lecture.

I'm tired of being lectured.

"I need to work with Mitzy a little more," I tell Gran. "Half an hour. I only have a little math."

"I doubt that," Gran answers. "I'll give you five more minutes."

Five minutes of freedom left.

As Gran closes the door, her cat, Socrates, squeezes out. Socrates is a big cat. He's a feline football fullback, all rust-colored fur and muscle. Gran named him after a Greek philosopher. He sure does lie around and think a lot. Sometimes he acts like he's guarding the clinic. Gran calls him a watchcat.

Socrates streaks across the yard, leaps onto the trunk of the old oak tree, and quickly claws his way up to a thick branch. Then he slinks along the branch and lies down where he can see the whole yard, like a lion watching the savanna.

"Show-off," I say under my breath. "Come here, Sherlock," I call. "Let's show Mitzy how to do it."

Sherlock gets up from his spot of shade and lumbers over to me, his long ears swinging and his tail wagging. Basset hounds are built low to the ground and can pick up smells easily. That's why I named him after a detective. Sherlock's nose is twitching, but everything must smell normal, because he comes right to me. He lifts his droopy eyelids expectantly.

"Sherlock, sit," I say in a firm voice.

Thump. His hindquarters hit the ground.

"Sherlock, lie down."

He stretches out his forelegs until he is lying down. He waits for the next command. Mitzy is watching us. I hope she's learning something.

"Stay." I jog to the far end of the yard. "Sherlock, come!"

He leaps to his feet and sprints toward me. Mitzy runs beside him. I kneel down and pet Sherlock. "You are the best dog in the world, aren't you? A genius, an absolute genius."

Mitzy puts her paw on my lap. When I reach for it, she rolls on her back.

"OK. You're a good dog, too, Mitz." I scratch her chest and she closes her eyes in contentment. "You just have to pay attention. You should watch old Sherlock here. He's a great teacher."

Suddenly both dogs prick up their ears and turn their heads toward the house. A car screeches into the parking lot next to the clinic.

Looks like we have a patient.

Chapter Two

- - - - - - - - - - - - -

The dogs dash to the front edge of the fence, with me close behind. We peek around the house. A frantic woman gets out of her car holding a limp puppy. She runs into the clinic.

"Sherlock! Mitzy! Come!" Sherlock comes right away. Mitzy plops her tail on the ground at the far end of the yard. Now she wants to sit.

There's only one thing to do. "Mitzy, lie down!" I command.

Mitzy jumps up and runs to the door. Maybe she's not stupid, after all. Maybe she's just a little confused.

When I herd the dogs inside, we're greeted by friendly barks from the boarding kennels. This is where we keep dogs whose owners are out of town. I put Mitzy in her cage and make sure she has fresh water to drink. She slurps, splashing water all over the floor. I'll have to remember to mop in here later.

Sherlock ambles toward the door that connects the clinic to the house, sniffing along the ground in hopes of discovering a hidden snack. Since he lives here and is the sweetest dog in the entire universe, he gets to go wherever he wants.

I walk to the front of the clinic, where there are two exam rooms—one on each side of the waiting room. Gran is talking to someone in the Dolittle Room. She named the exam rooms after veterinarians in her favorite books. I knock gently on the open door.

"Come in," Gran says.

Gran is a big woman, no matter how you look at her. She's taller than me—everyone's taller than me—and her hands and arms are strong. She wears bright colors, even when she's working in the clinic. Her hair is cut short enough that she can dry it with a towel, and I can't remember the last time she wore makeup. She's not a cookies-and-milk granny. She's a doctor—smart, tough, and kind. I love her lots.

"Take a look," she says.

I make notes to myself the way Gran taught me. Our patient is a black Labrador retriever. He looks like he's only two months old. Puppies this age are supposed to have nice fat tummies. This little guy is way too thin. He should be moving around, exploring everything. Instead, he lies on the table. His dark eyes are sunk into his head. That means he's dehydrated—he doesn't have enough fluid in his body. His coat is a dull black, dusted with white flakes. He probably has some kind of skin condition, too.

Gran works quickly. She uses a stethoscope to listen to his heart and lungs, then feels his abdomen with her hands. She tries to stand him up, but the little pup just collapses on the table. She peers into his mouth and eyes with a penlight. When she turns his head to examine one of his ears, he looks up at me with sad brown eyes. He's in pretty bad shape. I get a lump in my throat, but swallow it quickly. As Gran says, getting upset won't get the work done.

"When did you notice something was wrong?" Gran asks the owner.

The owner dabs a wet tissue at her eyes. "I've only had him two days. I bought him at the farmer's market on Penn Street. His name is Shelby."

When she says his name, the tears start again. I hand her a box of tissues.

"He was skinny and acted sleepy, but I thought he just needed some love. I went home an hour ago to check on him, and he was lying on the floor. He couldn't even lift up his head."

"Shelby's a sick pup, no question about that," Gran says. "I need to get some fluids into him and run some blood tests."

"Is he going to be OK?" the owner asks while shredding another tissue.

"He's malmourished, and he probably has worms in his intestines. I suspect he hasn't been vaccinated either. I'll know more about what's bothering him after I see the results of the tests."

"That doesn't sound good."

"Let's take it one step at a time. He'll have to spend the night here. I'll call you in the morning."

The owner runs her hands over Shelby's back. She bites her lip to hold back more tears.

"Don't worry," I say, leading her out of the exam room. "Gran is the best vet around. She'll do everything she can to save Shelby."

The woman nods, jots down her number, then leaves.

As soon as the door closes behind Shelby's owner, it bursts open again. A man rushes in holding a small cardboard box. Twin toddler boys clutch his pants, howling like someone stuck them with a pin.

Two identical black Lab puppies lie on a blanket in the box, fighting to breathe. They look just like Shelby.

"Please help us," the father says. "Something is terribly wrong."

Chapter Three

. . . .

The father and his wailing twins follow me into the exam room. Gran lifts an eyebrow. She doesn't mind loud animals, but she can't stand it when kids cry.

The father places the box on the table, and Gran looks in. "Take Shelby," she says to me. "I don't want him too close to these pups until we figure out what's wrong with them."

I gently pick Shelby up and carry him to the far side of the room. I make a safe, soft bed out of clean towels for him to rest in.

Gran squats in front of the crying twins. "Hi, guys. I'm Dr. Mac," she says. "I'm going to try to help your puppies. You can stay in here if you're quiet. If you need to cry, you have to wait in the other room. Fair?"

The twins nod their heads solemnly and blink away their tears. Gran is a magician.

After settling Shelby into his bed of towels, I wash my hands with antibacterial soap. I have the cleanest hands of any eleven-year-old I know. Gran is a fanatic about fighting germs.

Gran quickly cleans the exam table with disinfectant and dries it off. Then she takes the two little Labs out of the box. It's like Shelby all over again. The pups are scrawny. Their fur is matted and dull, and their eyes are crusty. The little one is breathing too fast, like he can't get enough air. Gran asks questions as she checks the pups.

"When were they born?"

"I don't know," the father says. "I bought them at the farmer's market last weekend. The boys saw them and fell in love. I didn't have a choice. The guy who sold them said they were old enough to be weaned."

"Vaccinations?"

"He didn't say."

"Did you see the mother?"

"No."

"Did you get any kind of health record?"

The father looks down at his shoes. "No. It was kind of an impulse buy, I guess. They were cute."

Gran doesn't answer. She's weighing the puppies.

"Did you get them at the Penn Street farmer's market?" I ask.

"Yes," answers the father. "How did you know?"

"That's where the little dog in the corner came from. I bet these two were sold by the same guy." I feel blood rushing to my face. I turn to Gran. "We should find out who he is. He shouldn't be selling sick puppies. Who knows how many more helpless pups he's got."

"Let's take care of our patients first," Gran answers calmly. "What are their names?" she asks the father.

"Inky and Dinky. Dinky is the smaller one."

"Dinky is my puppy," says one of the twins. His lower lip quivers, his face crumples, and he starts to cry again. His brother joins in.

"Maggie—" Gran starts.

"It's all right," the father interrupts. "I should take the boys home. Why don't you call me, Dr.

Mac? I'll leave my name and number at the front desk."

He does not look hopeful.

Once the twins and their father are gone, Gran asks me to gather the things she'll need to start an I.V., an intravenous drip.

"I need two bags of lactated Ringer's solution. Inky and Dinky need more fluid in their systems."

As I get the bags of Ringer's, Gran inserts a needle into a vein in each puppy's right foreleg. A thin plastic tube, called a catheter, is attached to the end of the needle. She connects each catheter to the bag of Ringer's solution. The solution looks like a bag of water, but it has special ingredients called electrolytes that the puppies need to help them get their energy back. Gran also gives them injections of antibiotics to help fight off infection.

"Will they make it?" I ask, worried.

"I don't know," she says. "It depends on how strong they are. Can you get me some charts, please? I need to write down my notes. I can't find anything since Lois left."

Lois, our last receptionist, quit last week. She was the third one this year, and it's only March.

Gran used to take care of all the paperwork by herself. But the clinic has gotten busier and she needs help. So far we haven't had any luck finding a receptionist who is not allergic to fur or afraid of birds.

The receptionist's desk is a nightmare. It's flooded with files and sticky notes. It looks like my desk upstairs. *Oh no—don't go there, Maggie. Desk means homework. Stay focused on the pups.*

I rummage through a desk drawer looking for the blank charts.

"Hello?" someone calls from the waiting room.

Chapter Four

● ● ● ● ● ● ● ● ● ● ● ●

A girl wearing a faded green "Save the Whales" sweatshirt leans over the reception counter. Her dark hair is pulled back in a long ponytail, and her earrings are shaped like howling wolves.

Boy, is she tall. I recognize her from school, and I've seen her here at the clinic before.

"Hi," I say. "Aren't you the girl with the pet crow?"

"That's me. Brenna Lake, reporting for duty. Dr. Mac told me I could start volunteering today. What do you need me to do first?"

A pile of folders slides off the desk and hits the floor. She's working here? Gran didn't tell me about this. There has to be some mistake.

"Um, I'm not sure. Let me get Gran."

Gran pokes her head in. "Maggie, I need those charts—oh, Brenna, you made it!" She walks around the desk. "Maggie, do you remember Brenna?"

"Yeah. She brought a crow in last fall. His name was Poe, right?"

"His full name is Edgar Allan Poe Crow, but we call him Poe. You have a good memory," Brenna says with a smile. She sticks her hands into the pockets of her jeans. She's wearing an old pair of boots, the kind that lace up the front. We look at each other, not quite sure what we should say next.

"Brenna's going to be working with us," Gran says. "She called last week with a question about Poe." Gran looks at the messy desk. "The day Lois quit."

I'm confused. "She's going to be our receptionist?"

"Not exactly," Gran says. She opens a file drawer and pulls out the blank charts she needs. "I had been thinking about bringing in a volunteer for a while. With Brenna around, you'll have more time for your homework."

Uh-oh. The H-word. Homework. I have a bad feeling about this.

"Brenna will help you with your clinic chores after school," Gran continues. "She can start right now. The cages need cleaning, and she can keep an eye on our newest patients. I've just moved them into the recovery room."

"But that's my job," I say. I can't believe Gran is bringing in someone with no experience to do it. I've been ambushed. This just isn't going to work, I can already see that.

Gran closes the file drawer and looks at me with a stern eye. "I want you to do your homework in the kitchen, Maggie. There are fewer distractions there."

I pick up the fallen files. I have to be smart about this. Temper tantrums don't work with my grandmother. She just ignores them.

"Now, Gran," I start. "I don't have that much homework. Besides, it's not fair to make Brenna do everything. Not on her first day."

"You're making excuses to get out of studying."

"I'm just worried about Brenna and the dogs. And you. You can't be everywhere at once, can you, Gran?"

The bells on the door jingle as another patient comes in. It's Mr. Asher, carrying Yertle, the turtle whose shell is too soft.

"I'll be right with you," Gran tells him.

"How about this? I'll do my homework in the recovery room. That way I can keep an eye on the puppies and answer Brenna's questions. What do you think?"

Brenna straightens a pile of business cards on the counter. "If you don't mind, Dr. MacKenzie, I'd like to have Maggie show me around a bit. It's my first day, and I have a lot of questions."

Gran looks at each of us. Brenna grins. I try on my most innocent expression.

"All right," she says. "Just for today. And you'll have to show me your homework after dinner."

Yes!

"Come on, Brenna. Follow me to the recovery room." I lift a section of the counter to let her into the back of the clinic.

• • • • • • •

Shelby, Inky, and Dinky are sleeping in a puppy pen on the floor of the recovery room. They look like little black commas curled around one another. A heat lamp shines over them, and their I.V. bags hang on a stand next to the pen.

"When a patient is recovering from surgery or from being real sick, they live in here," I explain to Brenna. "Gran is strict about keeping every-thing in the clinic spotless. Let me show you how to clean the cages."

A double-decker row of cages stands against the back wall. I open the first door and talk her through the steps of taking out the dirty news-papers that line the bottom, disinfecting and wiping the inside, then laying down clean news-paper.

Brenna catches on quickly. Too quickly. She cleans the second cage almost as fast as I did the first. Who knows what job of mine Gran will give her next? I'm going to have to have a talk with Gran.

"I can do the rest," she says. "You better get started on your homework."

I really don't like the way this is working out.

"Are you sure?" I ask. "Let me walk you through one more."

"Go on, Maggie. I don't want Dr. Mac to be angry on my first day here," Brenna explains.

"Yeah, yeah, yeah." I sigh. I'm going to talk to Gran *tonight*.

I drag out my backpack and flop on the floor with my humongous social studies book. "I have a test on government tomorrow. I'm supposed to memorize gigantic words like *legislation* and *subcommittee*."

Brenna takes dirty newspaper out of a cage and dumps it in a trash bag. "We had that test last week," she says. "It was easy. Make sure you know the steps of making a new law. We had to write an essay on that."

"Great." I turn the page and try to read.

Laws start with ideas. State representatives (another big word) vote on the new law. Blah, blah, blah. Every sentence has a word I trip over. I should look up the words I don't know, but that doesn't work either, because the definitions have words I don't understand. I read really slowly to begin with—throw in super-long words and I'll never finish.

My eyelids are drooping. I think I need a break. Brenna is on her fourth cage already. I close the book and sit up.

"Brenna, are you sure you haven't done this before?" I ask.

"Well, I did have to clean my crow's cage when he was really sick and lived inside the house," she says.

"What was wrong with him?"

Brenna spreads clean newspaper on a tray and slides it into a cage. "Jeez. You studied for two seconds. No wonder Dr. Mac asked me to come."

"I know this stuff. We saw a movie on it. Wait, you didn't spray it enough. Without the disinfectant, the inside of the cage can get moldy, really gross. And the germs could infect another animal. When a patient is in the recovery room, we want them to get better, not sick." I stand up. "Let me show you how to do it."

Brenna frowns and holds the disinfectant bottle out of my reach. "You already showed me. I don't want your grandmother coming in here and seeing you doing all the work."

"Just give it to me."

"No way."

We glare at each other like two stubborn mules. She sprays the tray and wipes it clean with a paper towel. "There. Is that good enough?"

"Yeah, I guess so. Make sure you scrub the corners—that's important." I think I may have met my match. I hand her fresh newspaper. "The crow. Tell me how you got Poe."

"I saw him get shot. I was walking in a field looking for red-shouldered hawks. I heard a gun go off and I hit the ground. Something fell near me. It was Poe."

"Somebody shot him? That's so sick."

"I jumped up hollering and they took off. They were kids, not much older than you and me, using a pellet gun. I took my jacket off, wrapped it around Poe, and carried him home. Dad drove me here. That was last fall. I thought we were going to be able to set him free, but his wing is wrecked. Before we knew it, he was one of the family."

"Your parents let you keep him?"

"It was my parents' idea."

"I'd like to meet them."

"They're pretty cool," she says as she closes the last cage. "All clean. Now what should I do?"

"It's definitely time to check the puppies."

We sit on the floor across from each other, with the puppies in the warm pen between us. Dinky is still breathing quickly, so I count the number of breaths per minute. One...two... three... He's OK. It's the same rate as earlier.

"Can I pet them?" Brenna asks quietly.

"Not yet," I say quickly. "We shouldn't dis-
turb them too much while they're on an I.V. See
how the fluid is dripping slowly?" I point out
the way the fluid drops into Dinky's tube.

"Is that bad or good?" Brenna asks.

"It's good in this case. It means he needs less
fluid. He's getting better."

"How do you know about all this stuff?"

"Gran taught me. I grew up here."

The phone rings once, then stops. Gran must
have picked it up.

"You live with Dr. Mac?" Brenna asks.

"Yep. My parents died in a car crash when I
was a baby."

"Oh. That's awful. I'm really sorry."

"It's OK. Gran's a good mom and a good
dad—not to mention a terrific grandmother.
This is the only home I remember."

Brenna leans closer to Dinky. "Maggie, this
one's shaking. Is that bad or good?"

I lightly rest my hand on his back. "Bad. He's
probably cold. Puppies this small get cold easily.
Believe it or not, it can kill them, especially if
they're already sick and malnourished. We need
to keep him warm because he's probably using

all his energy to fight off the infection." I pull a small blanket out of the cupboard. "This will help."

As I tuck the blanket around him, Dinky opens his tiny mouth and yawns, then snuggles his face against the palm of my hand. "Wow," Brenna says. "No wonder you're behind on your homework. You get to hang out with little critters like this!"

Gran comes through the door wearing her serious vet face—no smile, just sheer concentration.

Brenna jumps to her feet. "Hi, Dr. MacKenzie. Maggie was just teaching me about the I.V. stuff. The cages are all clean."

"Relax, relax," Gran says. "Anyone can clean cages. A veterinary clinic needs people who love animals. I wish I had more like you and Maggie."

"What's up?" I ask.

"A litter of sick puppies is on the way in," she says as she rubs her neck.

"Yikes. A whole litter? Is Dr. Gabe coming?" I ask.

"He's out vaccinating the Wilsons' goats," she

explains. "I'll try to find another vet or a vet technician to come in."

"What's wrong with the puppies?" I ask.

Gran pauses. "Who knows? It sounds like they're malnourished and wormy. I'll need some extra eyes and hands. I can't watch seven puppies at once." She holds the phone between her ear and shoulder and looks for a phone number in the directory. "You two can help. Wash up."

Chapter Five

· · · · · · · · · · ·

Gran hangs up the phone. "Bad news. Everyone is busy," she says. "Gabe is dealing with an emergency at the Wilsons' barn, so he'll be late. We're on our own."

"Do you really need another vet?" Brenna asks. "Maybe we just need a couple more people to help watch the puppies."

Gran nods. "You're right. But I need them now." She takes the phone book back out of the drawer and flips it open.

"Who are you calling?" I ask.

"David. David Hutchinson from across the

street. He's been pestering me about volunteering."

"Please, Gran, I'm begging you. Not David!"

Gran points at a number on the page and dials the phone. "It's time to give him a chance. He has grown up a bit."

"But . . . he's a goofball. He's a klutz—"

"He's enthusiastic. And he's close."

Two minutes later, David gallops into the clinic as if he had been waiting for the call. His bangs flop in front of his eyes. He's wearing a hockey jersey, the same pair of jeans he has worn every day for the past year, and sneakers. Untied, of course.

"Hey, what's up, Dr. Mac? Finally decided you couldn't live without me? Or is it Maggie who needs my help?"

David steps toward me. My hands curl into fists.

"Maybe not!" He backs away.

"This is Brenna Lake," Gran says. "She's helping out, too."

"David and I are in the same class," Brenna says with a sigh. "We did a science project together. He almost set the table on fire."

"It was a small explosion," David explains. "I had it all under control. Did you finish the homework?" he asks Brenna.

"I did it on the bus," she answers. "Do you have to pay for the broken microscope?"

"You broke a microscope?" I ask. Typical. David can't walk to the bus stop without causing damage. Gran is nuts to let him in here. What is she thinking?

"OK, everyone, you can chitchat later. Put these on." Gran hands us scrub tops.

"Hey, cool!" David says. "These are just like the ones real docs wear."

"David, you need to wash your hands, and yes, you have to use soap. And scrub your nails," Gran says.

The bells on the front door jingle. Brenna jumps up and David spins around.

It's not the lady with the litter of sick puppies. It's Sunita Patel, her arms loaded down with books she borrowed from Gran.

Sunita is one of the quietest kids in Ambler,

Pennsylvania. She's about my size, with chocolate brown eyes and long black hair. Her parents are from India. They're both doctors—human doctors. Anyway, she's wearing a typical Sunita outfit: loafers, khakis, and a purple turtleneck. She looks good in purple because her skin is a beautiful light brown color, like milky tea. If I wear purple, I look like I'm going to barf.

"Hello, Dr. MacKenzie?" she says with a shy smile. "I just came to return the books you lent me. Thanks. Sorry for interrupting." She puts the books on the counter and then turns to leave.

"Stay, Sunita," Gran says. "I'm collecting volunteers, and we could use your help." She explains to her what we're all waiting for.

"I don't know," Sunita says. "I'm not sure I'll be much help."

"C'mon. It'll be fun. And you'll get to wear one of these," David says, tugging on his scrub top.

"It's not supposed to be fun," Brenna argues. "It's serious."

I jump in. "Gran needs our help. Will you stay, Sunita? Please?"

She nods and smiles. "All right. But I have to

be home in time for dinner." She sits on one of the plastic chairs. "What do you want me to do?"

"I need your eyes," Gran says. "I need everyone's eyes," she repeats, louder.

The rest of us take a seat. Gran has center stage.

"There are seven puppies coming in. I can't examine seven at once," she explains. "I'll decide who is the sickest, who I have to treat first. All of you need to keep an eye on the other pups. If you notice any change—if they breathe faster or slower, if they shake or stop shaking, if they drool, if their eyelids flutter—tell me immediately. Are you up to it?"

David looks serious for a change. Sunita is alert. Brenna's knee bounces up and down. I'm up to it—I was born ready to take care of animals like this. We all nod.

Brenna turns to the window. "They're here!"

Chapter Six

. . . .

A woman carries two large picnic baskets into the clinic. Gran hustles her straight back to the Dolittle Room. The woman sets the baskets on the table, and we all crowd around for a look. Gran opens the baskets. Inside are six tiny collies only a few weeks old, plus a mutt—a mixed-breed.

Gran gently pulls up the skin of one of the pups. It falls back into place too slowly. "Looks like they're dehydrated," explains Gran. "Let's get each pup a bed. Maggie, fill some surgical gloves with warm water so we can rest the pups on them. Brenna, roll that O_2 canister over here."

"Maggie!" Brenna whispers. "What's O_2?"

"Oxygen. Let me show you." I roll the small canister of oxygen to Gran. "We'll need a small mask since we're dealing with puppies here." I hook up a mask to the tubing. "See? It's easy."

"For you, maybe."

"Here, help me with the beds," I say to Brenna, David, and Sunita. I show them how to fill surgical gloves with warm water, tie them off, and line them up on the counter. Then we cover them with towels.

"Ready, Gran," I shout.

"All right!" Gran says briskly. "I'll take a puppy out of the basket, look it over quickly, and hand it to Maggie. Maggie will bring it over to you. Then you stand guard over the pups. Here we go."

Gran takes one of the larger pups out and hands it to me. He's shaking, just like Dinky did earlier. I carefully carry him to Brenna and set him on his warm bed. He lets out a weak whimper. Brenna stands close to the counter, her hands on either side of the puppy, protecting him and making sure he doesn't crawl away.

"Next!" calls Gran.

I take the next patient, the mutt, to David, then return for another one.

As Gran hands over the pups, the owner tells us what she knows. "I found them crowded into a dirty cage at the farmer's market yesterday," she says. "They didn't have any food or water, and they were filthy. Whenever they whined, the owner yelled at them and rattled the cage until they stopped."

It's the same guy who sold Shelby, Inky, and Dinky. I just know it.

"Let me guess," Gran says. "He didn't give you any health information, no papers, no nothing."

"He was mad that I even asked questions about their health. We argued," the owner admits. "I threatened to report him to the Humane Society for abusing the dogs. It was obvious they were sick. He picked up the cage and walked away from me."

"Then how did you get the puppies?" Sunita asks.

"I followed him. When we got to his truck, I took out my wallet. I gave him all the cash I had. I just couldn't let him take them away."

"Good for you!" Brenna says.

"So you rescued these puppies yesterday?" Gran asks, gently pulling the last puppy out of the basket.

The owner blushes. "I know. I should have called you right away. I thought the little guys just needed a clean, warm home and some food. I was going to make an appointment this week-end, but then the shaking and diarrhea started."

"Are you going to keep all of them?" David asks.

"No. I can't. I thought if I cleaned them up, I could find good homes for them."

Gran hands me the last puppy. I'm going to watch over this one. Brenna, David, and Sunita stand in a line along the counter, all carefully watching over two puppies each.

Gran strides over to check on Sunita's collie. "This one wins first place." She puts her stetho-scope against his chest. We all watch in silence, as if we're listening for the pup's heartbeat, too.

"He's breathing fast and his lungs are con-gested." Gran presses her fingertips against the inside of the pup's hind leg. "Pulse is fast and weak. His heart is struggling. Maggie, take his temperature."

David shifts over to watch my puppy in addi-

tion to his two so I can help Gran. I lift the collie's tail and insert a thermometer. I think he's
too sick to notice. Gran is looking in his mouth.

"He's anemic. See how his gums are white?
They should be pink." Her hands glide over the
puppy's tiny body, checking for other clues to
what is making him sick.

I remove the thermometer and read it aloud.
"One hundred and five."

"That's what we call a fever," Gran observes.

Brenna is shocked. "He has a temperature of
one hundred and five degrees? I thought that
could kill you."

"The normal temperature for a dog is between
100 and 102.5 degrees," I explain. "A temperature of 105 is high, but it's not really, really
high."

Brenna strokes the two puppies in front of her.
"I guess it's hard to tell just by touching them,
isn't it? Is this one too hot?"

"Hang on," Gran says to Brenna. "I'll be there
in a second."

"I heard that if a dog's nose is dry, it means he
has a fever," David says.

"That's just an old wives' tale," Gran explains.
"The only way you can take a dog's temperature

is to use a thermometer. Maggie, could you get me some Ringer's solution?"

I grab a bag of the clear fluid and set it where Gran can reach.

"He's dangerously dehydrated. These fluids will replace what he has lost from the diarrhea," she says, hooking the solution up to a tube that leads to the pup.

"Hand me that syringe, Maggie." Gran points to a plastic tube with a needle on one end and a plunger on the other. I hand it to her—carefully. She fills it with medicine, then gently but swiftly inserts the needle into the pup's foreleg. "This is an antibiotic to help fight the infection," she explains, pushing down on the plunger. "Next!"

I push the instrument cart behind Gran as she walks down to where David is standing and examines the mutt.

"I bet the mother of these puppies is sick, too," I say. "Plus, the guy at the farmer's market was selling different breeds. Collies and Labs. It's a puppy mill, Gran. I know it. We've got to do something."

"What's a puppy mill?" David asks.

Gran draws a vial of blood from the mutt.

"A puppy mill is a place where dogs are bred in unhealthy conditions. Puppy mills are illegal and unethical. The people who run them spend as little as possible to raise the pups so they can make a profit when they sell them. They are horrible places for dogs, run by people who care only about money."

My blood starts to boil just listening to Gran. Who could do such a thing?

"We have to shut it down and rescue the other dogs!" Brenna says, joining my cause.

"I wish I had the time, Brenna," Gran says, giving the mutt an injection of antibiotics. "I'll call the animal shelter and tell them what we have here. They probably don't have enough staff to search for the puppy mill owner, but they can watch for other pups."

David cranes his neck to see what Gran is doing. He loses his balance and bumps into the instrument cart. Everything crashes to the ground. The noise startles the puppies and a few of them yip. Everybody stares at David.

"Sorry," he says with a shrug. "I'll try to be more careful."

Great. Now I'll have to sterilize those instruments again. I quickly get Gran a new instrument pack and pick up the mess on the floor.

"Maggie, will you look at my puppies," Brenna asks.

"They're fine," I assure her. "See? Their chests are moving up and down, and they're warm enough. You're doing a great job."

I look over at Sunita. Her eyes are huge. "Oh—oh my," she gasps.

"Don't faint," Brenna commands. "Nobody has a free hand to catch you."

"I won't faint," Sunita says. "But one of my puppies just had diarrhea, and there is a lot of blood in it."

I grab some towels and help clean Sunita's puppy.

"Yech," says David. He leans down to the puppies he's watching. "Don't you do that, OK? Promise?"

"Maggie, we're going to need fecal samples," says Gran.

That means I should save the messy towels from Sunita's pup so Gran can study the feces under a microscope for germs.

"They can't die from this, can they?" asks David.

"Yes, they can," I say.

"Oh, gee." David tilts his head so his puppies can see him better. "No dying, got that? No
pooping, no dying."

"Maggie, can you check my pups again?"
Brenna asks.

I bounce from dog to dog, from kid to kid.
Gran works to stabilize the patients. Sunita,
Brenna, and David concentrate on the little
chests in front of them. The owner stands in the
corner, watching our every move. It feels like
time is frozen. I am totally focused.

"Dr. Mac!" Brenna calls suddenly.

Gran and I rush over to see what's wrong. One
of the collies is shaking violently.

Gran listens to the puppy's heartbeat, then
calls for the oxygen mask. But before I can get to
her, the puppy goes completely still. Gran feels
for a pulse, then closes her eyes.

She didn't find one.

"I'm sorry," she says. "There was nothing we
could have done to save him. The infection was
too strong."

Tears cloud my eyes and my stomach drops
to my shoes. Sunita and David look at the floor.
Brenna holds her breath.

Poor pup. He had such a short life. I wonder

how many others are—I can't think about it now. I have to help Gran. I sniff and wipe my nose on my sleeve.

"Can I take him home to bury him?" the owner asks.

Gran nods. I wrap the tiny collie in a clean towel and hand him over. He's still, but peaceful.

"All right, deep breath, everybody," Gran commands. "It's hard when animals die, but we're all doing our best. If any of you want to leave, you can. I'll understand."

"I'm not leaving," Brenna declares. "I'm here to help."

"I can't leave," says David. "These guys need me. The puppies, I mean, not you guys. I mean, you girls." He stutters. "You know what I mean."

We all turn to Sunita. She is crouched over her messy collie, her hand resting gently on its back. She looks up.

"He's hardly breathing, Dr. Mac!"

Gran wheels the oxygen canister over. She turns it on, slips the oxygen mask over his snout, then listens with her stethoscope. She gives his chest a gentle push. "Come on, come on," she mutters. "You can do it." Another push. The collie takes a little breath, then a deeper one. "That's it, nice and easy."

We all relax. He's going to make it.

Once all the puppies have been examined and treated, Gran and I move them to a special oxygen cage in the recovery room, where it will be easier for them to breathe. Then we all stand together, eyes glued on our patients. It's like when people crowd around the window in the maternity ward. We feel connected to these dogs.

Our moment of silence ends when the front door slams shut. We hear whistling. "Dr. Gabe is back," I explain. "He works here with Gran and me. He's the associate veterinarian."

"And he'll take over from here," Gran interrupts. "I am officially relieving all of you of your duties. All our patients need now is some peace and quiet. Gabe and I will take good care of them, don't you worry."

I wait for her to thank the others and say they can go home now. They were helpful, but it feels kind of weird to have all these kids around.

But then Gran says, "Maggie, take them into the kitchen for a snack. I'm sure everyone's hungry."

Chapter Seven

• • • • • • • • • • •

"Cool!" Brenna says as we walk into the kitchen.

I love this room. It is in the oldest part of the house. Gran combined the original dining room and the kitchen into one giant room with a fireplace and a couch, along with the normal stuff like tables, chairs, and a microwave. A sliding glass door looks out onto the patio and the backyard. It's the best part of the house, without a doubt.

David stretches out on the couch. "You can bring me my grapes now." Brenna throws a pillow at his head. "Ow!"

"Do you want some help?" Sunita asks me.

I scan the pantry. "There's not a lot to eat," I say over the noise of Brenna and David's pillow fight. "But we have plenty of dog biscuits."

"You've got to have something else," says David as a pillow sails over his head. "How about some ice cream or chocolate-covered pretzels?"

"Dog biscuits, liver treats… hang on, I'm still looking. Boy, do we need to go shopping."

"Some people like the way dog biscuits taste," Sunita says.

The pillow fight stops. We all stare at her.

"Not me," she says, blushing. "I read it in a magazine. Really."

"I believe you," I say. "Let me try the cupboard. We have pasta, canned peas, oatmeal…" I move the oatmeal container aside. "Aha! The last of the Girl Scout cookies!"

"That's more like it," says David.

There aren't too many cookies, so I take a jar of pickles out of the fridge and set that on the table, too. I love pickles.

"I'll take the Thin Mints," David says. He crams two cookies in his mouth.

I whistle and Sherlock trots into the kitchen. I toss him a dog biscuit.

"Well, he certainly looks healthy," says Sunita

as she wipes cookie crumbs off her mouth.

"Sherlock is never sick," I say. "He's sort of our mascot. We have a cat, too, named Socrates. Wait until you see him—he's the boss."

"It must be so wonderful to be surrounded by animals every day," Sunita says with a sigh. "What's the best part about living here?"

"I never really thought about it." I take a bite of pickle. "I guess I like getting to know our patients. Animals are like people to me. Sometimes they are better than people. You know what I mean?"

David nods. "You can trust them."

"And they trust you," adds Sunita.

"They all have personalities, and most of them are fun. It's great to watch Gran make a sick animal feel better, or help owners understand how to take care of their pets."

"There must be bad parts, though," Brenna says.

"The worst part is when an owner doesn't treat a pet properly. And it's hard not to get upset and cry when animals die. But it is such a rush to help animals and their owners—that makes up for the sad times. I'm definitely going to be a veterinarian when I grow up."

"Which is why you should do your homework," Brenna points out.

"Please! I'm eating."

"What's wrong with homework?" Sunita asks.

"Maggie hates it. She's kind of grounded because she keeps blowing it off," Brenna explains. She pulls a pickle out of the jar. "That's why I'm here. Dr. Mac asked me to help with some of Maggie's chores in the clinic." I flash her a look and she freezes with the pickle halfway to her mouth. "At least for a while," she adds.

Sunita takes a pickle, too. "I wish I could come here every day."

David slaps his forehead.

"Brainstorm!" he shouts. "I'm a genius."

"Yeah, right," I say. The girls laugh.

"No, listen," he says. "This is a really good idea. We should all volunteer here. We could come after school and on the weekends."

"Awesome," Brenna says.

Awful.

"Could we?" asks Sunita.

They stare at me like golden retrievers begging for a walk.

"I don't know," I begin. "We're sort of used to

doing things on our own around here."

"No, really, Maggie. We'd make a great team!" Brenna says. "Think about it. I'm strong and not afraid to get dirty. Sunita is friendly and smart. Now, David. What would he do?"

David makes a face and Sunita giggles.

Brenna nods. "OK. He's good for a laugh now and then. And we're all nuts about animals. Look at how great we handled the puppies that came in today. We'll be like junior vets or something!"

"You did help with the puppies," I say. "That worked out OK, I guess..."

"Of course it did," Brenna says. "Now we need a plan. We have to show Dr. Mac that she needs us every day."

"We don't need a plan," David says. "Dr. Mac loves us."

Brenna and Sunita look at each other and crack up.

"Are you always this optimistic?" Sunita asks.

"You mean unrealistic," Brenna says.

"You have to think positive," David says. "Like with my mom, whenever I ask for anything, I assume she's going to say yes."

"Does it work?" Sunita asks.

"Well . . . not always," David admits. "But it's worth trying." He leans back. "It's going to work. I know it. Dr. Mac is a smart lady. She's not going to say no to volunteers like us. I'm seeing a very nice future."

That's not what I see. I see trouble.

I get up from the table and rummage in the cupboard for a napkin so the others can't see my face. I hope Gran says no. We don't need their help around here—not even Brenna's. Gran has me. I'm not a real vet, but I know how to do all the little stuff. This is my place. I don't want anyone else around.

"What do you think, Maggie?" Sunita asks.

Luckily for me, the phone rings just then. "Hang on, guys." I pick it up. "Hello?"

There is no response. Brenna laughs at something David says. I turn my back to them and cover my ear so I can hear better.

"Hello?" I say again louder.

"Maggie? This is your aunt Rose."

"Oh, hi, Aunt Rose." Rose is my father's sister. She and Gran hardly ever talk. They don't get along. Aunt Rose and her daughter, Zoe—my cousin—live in New York City. Rose is an actress in a soap opera or something.

"How are you?" she asks. Her voice is smooth, like the announcer on a shampoo commercial.

"Fine." Not really. "How are you?"

"Fabulous. I've been offered a role, a leading role, in a new TV sitcom. I'm leaving for Los Angeles tomorrow."

"Um, congratulations."

Brenna says something to the others, and they run back to the clinic.

"Do you want to talk to Gran?"

"Yes, thank you."

I set the phone down and call Gran on the intercom to pick up.

I have a funny feeling about this.

Chapter Eight

. . . .

When Gran picks up, I hang up the phone and look at Sherlock. "I bet they're in the clinic right now waiting to ask Gran if they can all volunteer. What am I going to do? How do I tell her that I don't want their help?"

He ignores me and vacuums up the cookie crumbs that David dropped.

I reach down and scratch between his ears. "I can't exactly kick them out, can I?"

Before I can get an answer, I hear a loud thump from the waiting room. "Rrruff!" growls Sherlock. He rumbles toward the door.

"I'm right behind you," I call, pushing open the swinging door to the waiting room.

That noise was a large plant tipping over. It's lying, roots and all, on the floor. David and Brenna are standing in the dirt on either side of it.

David points at the mess. "It's your fault, Brenna. You clean it up."

"My fault!" Brenna yells. She's steamed. "I'm not picking this up. I didn't do anything! You were the one pretending to be a ballerina."

Sunita can see how confusing this is to me. "I told them that I took ballet, and then David had to prove he could dance. He pirouetted right into the plant."

"At least I missed the window."

"You still have to clean it up," says Brenna.

"It wasn't my fault! You were standing in the way."

"Somebody better do something quickly," Sunita warns. "Dr. Mac's next patient is coming up the walk."

David grabs the plant, Brenna pushes the pot under a chair, and I scoop up the dirt with my hands just as Mrs. Cooper walks through the front door with a yowling cat carrier.

"Hello, Mrs. Cooper! How is Ling Ling today?" I ask, holding a handful of dirt.

"Meerow." A light brown paw pushes through the wire door of the cat carrier. Sunita melts.

"A Siamese! Oh, how beautiful! I love Siamese cats." She touches the paw with the tip of her finger.

"Meerow! Meerow!" Ling Ling cries. Siamese are the most talkative kind of cat.

"Sunita, why don't you take Mrs. Cooper and Ling Ling into the Herriot Room, over there on the left. I'll tell Gran that you're here, Mrs. Cooper."

"Thank you, Margaret," says Mrs. Cooper. Sunita grins. She escorts cat and owner to the exam room.

"Margaret? I thought you flattened people who call you Margaret," David says as soon as Sunita closes the door to the Herriot Room.

"I'll flatten you if you don't fix that plant."

He plops the plant back in the pot. "There, all fixed. Happy?"

I dump the dirt I'm holding back into the pot. "Happy." I buzz Gran on the intercom to let her know that Ling Ling is here.

"Now who do I pay to get a tour around here?" asks David.

"A tour?"

"Why not? It was so busy when the collies came in, I never got to see behind the scenes."

"OK, but it'll be a short tour, and no ballet moves. This is obviously the waiting room. Sunita just went into the Herriot Room. Across from that is the Doolittle Room. That's where we usually examine dogs."

"I know who Dr. Doolittle is. I read a book about him. But what does Herriot mean?" asks Brenna.

"James Herriot was the pen name of an English veterinarian, Dr. James Alfred Wight. Gran loves his books. *All Creatures Great and Small* is one of her favorites. Next stop, the receptionist's desk." I flip up the counter. "There's a computer under this mess somewhere. We're having a hard time finding an animal-friendly receptionist. They always leave after a day or two."

"I know. I was on my bike when one of them ran out of the clinic screaming," says David. "What was she so afraid of?"

"A skunk. A pet skunk. He couldn't spray anymore, but she took one look and never returned. Follow me."

Past the desk is the hallway that leads to the hospital part of the clinic. I open the door to the operating room. "This is where surgery takes place. Notice the shiny equipment. Don't touch, David." We walk through the operating room to the recovery room.

"Hi, Dr. Gabe. How are the puppies?"

"Sleeping soundly. No problems. Dr. Mac told me what a great job you kids did," he says.

"Dr. Mac and Maggie did all the work," says Brenna. "We just did what they told us to do."

"Well, you listened. That's more than a lot of people do."

"I'm giving them a tour," I tell Gabe, then turn back to David and Brenna. "This is the recovery room, where we watch animals recovering from surgery or sickness. Those cages on the back wall"—I point—"usually have an assortment of critters in them, rabbits, ferrets, dogs—"

"Cows," Dr. Gabe teases.

"No, we don't keep cows in here. Ignore him. Now to our left, you'll see a real live veterinarian. We call this creature Dr. Gabriel Donovan.

Don't be afraid. He's scruffy looking, but he doesn't bite."

Dr. Gabe snaps his teeth at us and barks. Brenna giggles. He is cute, but I can't have a crush on him because he's way too old, like twenty-eight or something. Dr. Gabe's been working here for years. He started volunteering when he was in high school and came back to be Gran's associate when he graduated from veterinary school. I better move on before Brenna falls under the spell of his ice blue eyes.

"Let's go. Take good care of the pups, Gabe."

"Mooooo," he replies.

We leave the recovery room and move on to the lab. "This is where we analyze blood, urine, and fecal specimens."

"Don't let David touch the microscope," Brenna suggests.

"Good idea. The next room is X-ray, followed by... the Beauty Shop. Gran has talked about hiring a groomer to work here, but she hasn't had time to set it up yet. Sometimes I groom a boarder in here."

"I had no idea this place was so big," Brenna says. "You can't tell from the front, can you?"

"A vet clinic is kind of like a small version of a

hospital. You need everything from labs to laundry machines."

"Oh, sure," David says. "Next you'll tell me you have a cafeteria."

"Of course. Animals with different illnesses require special diets. We provide those, too," I explain. "And guess who's the head waitress?"

"OK, so the next time a kitty wants dessert, can you bring her a three-*mouse*keteer bar?" David doubles over with laughter.

Brenna and I groan.

"Gran has the latest equipment and supplies so she can give our patients the care they deserve," I say, getting back to the subject.

"Jeez! This place must have cost a fortune." That's David's way of asking where the money is coming from. I think we're lucky to have the setup we do. Gran has worked really hard for it all.

"Gran writes a column about animals that appears in newspapers all over the country, and she's published a bunch of books. A few years ago, she invented a couple of surgical tools. She gets extra money from that, too. Come on. Tour's almost over."

I lead them through the door to the boarding kennels. "Gran keeps the boarders separate from the sick animals in the recovery room so the boarders won't be exposed to germs."

"Rrrouf!" Mitzy stands by the door to her kennel and barks for attention.

"Hi, Mitzy." I reach in and pet my student. "We have room for ten dogs. Each one gets an inside cage like this, and they have their own runs—long, fenced-in areas where they can romp around. We don't have too many right now, but you should see this place in the summer." I stand up and brush my hands on my jeans. "OK. That's it. Tour's over."

"No, it's not," David says. "We passed a couple of doors that you didn't open."

"We want to see everything," Brenna says.

"Follow me." I sigh. We leave Mitzy behind and go back to the main hall. I put my hand on the doorknob of one of the "mystery" doors. "This is the supply closet. To open it is to take your life in your hands. It is so messy, it makes my room look neat, and that is saying something."

David scoots ahead of me and opens the last door. "What's in here? Yikes!"

"What is it?" asks Brenna.

I peek in. "This is Gran's office. The extremely large creature on Gran's desk is Socrates."

"Wow!" exclaims Brenna.

Socrates looks at Brenna and closes his eyes once. He is pleased with her admiration.

"He rules the roost. He thinks that we are his pets, or maybe his servants. Our job is to feed him."

"You make it sound like he's a snob," says Brenna.

"Well, he's not cuddly, that's for sure. And if he's guarding Gran's office, I'm not going in there. Come on, let's go back up front."

• • • • • • • •

By the time we make our way to the waiting room, Ling Ling is yowling on her way to the car. Gran and Sunita are standing at the door.

"You did an amazing job keeping her calm," Gran tells Sunita. "Ling Ling needed eardrops," she explains to us.

"So how many scratches did you get?" I ask. Ling Ling does not like eyedrops.

"No scratches. Sunita has a real gift with cats."

"Well," I say, "I guess you guys have to get home for dinner."

"Oh, my goodness," Sunita says, looking at her watch. "My parents don't like me to be late. Thank you very much, Dr. MacKenzie. This was the best day I've had in ... in ... in a very long time." She heads out the door.

"Hey guys. Wait," David says. "We didn't ask about tomorrow."

"What about tomorrow?" Gran asks.

"Can Sunita and I come back? To help?"

There's a long pause. I look at Gran. I can see she's thinking it over.

Please say no, Gran. Please say no.

"Thank you, but that won't be necessary. We have Brenna here to help, and we're over the real crisis. We just need to monitor the pups from here on out. But I couldn't have done without you today. You were all great."

Whew. Saved.

Brenna buckles on her bike helmet and hops on her bike. David shuffles out the door and cuts through the hedge without looking back. Sunita walks down the driveway. At the sidewalk, she turns and waves to us with a faint smile. I wave back.

Gran looks like she's a thousand miles away. She sure is acting strange.

"Is something wrong?" I ask. "You know I'll pull my grades up. Pretty soon, you won't even need Brenna to do my work."

Gran leans against the doorframe and crosses her arms over her chest. "It's not just that. It's your aunt Rose. Remember her phone call? Her daughter, Zoe, is coming tomorrow." She picks some cat hair off her sleeve. "She'll be staying with us for a while."

The pickles twist in my stomach. "What? How long is a while?" The last time I saw Zoe was a year ago. We didn't get along so well.

"Maybe a couple of weeks until her mom gets settled in L.A. I insisted we enroll her in school. And I'm counting on you to show her around and make her feel comfortable. We'll talk more about it after I finish up in the clinic. Now, don't you have a test to study for?"

Chapter Nine

. . . .

I studied for the social studies test. Honest. But it was a waste of time. I got a miserable, rotten 57 percent. D minus. My teacher graded it right in front of me. I hate social studies. I hate tests. I hate school. Now I have to go home and tell Gran. She's going to explode when she sees it. How can I make her believe I really tried?

David sits next to me on the bus and asks all kinds of questions about the puppies. Great. Now, on top of having to break the news to Gran, I start worrying about the puppy mill again.

As we step off the bus, it starts to rain. "Say hi to the pups," shouts David, crossing the street.

"You know where to find me if you need any help over there."

In your dreams.

Everyone else runs for home holding their backpacks over their heads to keep dry. I walk slowly through the downpour.

What am I going to say to Gran? Maybe she'll forget to ask about it.

When I open the back door to the clinic, the dogs in the kennel start yipping. Now that's a warm sound. I hang up my dripping jacket and go straight to the recovery room to check on our patients. The collies and the mutt are out of the oxygen cage. That's great. It means they are breathing better on their own. They are in a puppy pen next to the one with the black Labs. Shelby and Inky look stronger, but I'm worried about Dinky, the smallest Lab. I check his chart. He has lost weight.

I hold Dinky up to my face. He opens his sleepy eyes. "What's wrong with you, little guy? You need to get big and strong, or your brother is going to get all the attention. You probably have more brothers and sisters at the puppy mill, don't you? Are they cold and hungry, too?" I get goose bumps.

Dinky doesn't answer—not even a wag of the tail. I'd love to hold him the rest of the afternoon, but he needs quiet to recover. I give him a kiss on the top of his head and settle him back in with Shelby and Inky.

I stop to count. Three Labs, five collies... Wait—where did the mutt go? My heart pounds.

I get on my hands and knees to search.

I look under the instrument cart. Not there.

I check behind the trash can. Nope.

There he is, crawling toward the door!

"You! You are sneaky," I scold as I scoop him up gently and carry him back to his pen. "Now don't you disappear on me again."

"Maggie?" Gran calls from down the hall.

"I'll be right there."

I put the mutt in the pen with the collies, then carefully close the door behind me on my way out.

• • • • • • •

Gran is in the Doolittle Room peering into the ears of a messy dog named Brigitte. Brigitte looks like a Yorkshire terrier, more or less. The hair inside her ears is caked with dried earwax and dirt.

"Yuck. Are they infected?" I ask.

"I'll know for sure once I can get a look in there. First I have to clean them out." Gran lays out the equipment she needs. "How did your test go?"

She doesn't forget anything.

"You don't want to know," I answer.

"That bad, huh?"

There is no way out. I take the test paper out of my backpack and hand it over. My teacher, Ms. Griffith, wrote her phone number on the front of it and a note asking Gran to call her.

Gran glances at the grade and looks across at me, tapping her fingers on the metal examination table. The noise makes Brigitte jumpy.

"Dial the phone," she says.

"Now? You're going to talk to Ms. Griffith now? You're working. You have to help Brigitte. And I haven't even explained what happened. There was all this stupid legal stuff on the test that she never talked about in class, and—"

"Call your teacher, and put her on speakerphone."

Ms. Griffith picks up on the first ring. Gran

introduces herself and starts to trim the matted hair in Brigitte's ears. Normally Brigitte is easy to work with, but today she's acting hyper, as if she just ate a giant bowl of sugarcoated cereal.

"I just don't know what to tell you, Dr. MacKenzie. Margaret pays attention in class, but when it comes to written work, or to tests, it's as though she's never heard the material before. I have tried everything." Ms. Griffith's voice crackles over the speakerphone. "I really think she needs a tutor—and to spend more time on her studies."

Brigitte twists her head away from Gran.

"Settle down!" Gran says.

"Excuse me?" Ms. Griffith asks.

I bite my lip and pet Brigitte.

"I'm very concerned about Margaret," Ms. Griffith continues. "If she fails the class, she'll have to repeat it in summer school. I've tried to talk to her several times, but I don't think she realizes how serious the situation is."

Gran picks up the otoscope to look into Brigitte's ears. Brigitte yelps and flinches before Gran touches her. She's really nervous.

"Don't get so worked up," says Gran, still talking to Brigitte.

"Excuse me, Dr. MacKenzie, but I am worked up, and with good cause!" says Ms. Griffith.

This would be funny if they weren't talking about such a serious subject—me. Eventually, Gran gets two things accomplished: she gets a good look at Brigitte's ear canals, and she agrees with Ms. Griffith about my torture—I mean my extra-credit assignment. I have to write a report about how laws are made.

After Ms. Griffith hangs up, Gran focuses on Brigitte. She flushes the infection out of her ears and puts in some medicine. Then she combs and trims the silky hair falling in her eyes.

I take a brush out of the cupboard and start on the tangles on her back. This poor little thing looks like she hasn't been brushed in months.

"Stop," Gran says. She takes the brush from my hand. "I've made a decision."

This does not sound good. I want to whine like Brigitte.

"You're grounded, Maggie MacKenzie. Double-dog grounded."

"But—"

"You can't help out in the clinic until you write that extra-credit report and get a good grade on it. And we are getting you a tutor."

"But, Gran, that's not fair. I already have to spend all day in school. You're going to make me go to a tutor, too?"

"Can you bring your grades up on your own?"

"Yes, I think I can. I just need to work harder, which I will. I promise, Gran, I promise."

Gran looks at me over her reading glasses. "All right. No tutor for now, then. But your grades have to come way up. Not a D, not a C. You have to get a B or better. And I don't want you in the clinic. I'm keeping you on a short leash until you prove yourself."

No clinic? No way. This is not fair.

"You can't do that. I mean, you can do it, but you need me. Who's going to walk dogs, pet cats, talk to snakes, or take care of whatever hops in tomorrow? I belong here, Gran. Please don't do this."

"I already have." She clips the hair matted around Brigitte's paws. "David had a good idea yesterday. I'm going to take him up on it. He and Sunita can help Brenna with your jobs. I'll call them when I'm done with Brigitte and ask them to come right over. Brenna should be here any minute now."

She trims the hair on Brigitte's tail. "Aside from freeing you up to concentrate on school-work, I think it might be nice to have some extra kids around. You know, for Zoe, so she can make some friends."

I'm sputtering, stuttering, and getting Yorkshire terrier fur in my mouth when Brenna walks in, whistling like a canary.

"I'm ready to work," she says.

"Be with you in a minute," Gran says. "Wash your hands." She picks up Brigitte. "Maggie, write down what Brenna has to feed Mitzy and the other boarders. Make a chart. When that's done, get started on correcting your test."

"Gran, you haven't let me say anything!"

Gran holds up her hand. "There is nothing to say. D minus is just not good enough, Maggie. If helping out in the clinic interferes with school-work, then you have to cut back on time spent here. With Brenna and the others around, it's a win-win situation."

Ha. It's a lose-lose situation, if you ask me.

• • • • • • •

Brenna follows me to the boarding kennels,

where I show her the cupboard that contains the food bowls and giant bags of dry food.

"Each dog gets fresh water, and the older dogs get a special feed. We aren't boarding any puppies, so you don't have to worry about them. Regular-size dogs like Mitzy get two and a half scoops of dry food and four little dog biscuits a day. If we had a big dog, like a Great Dane, it could eat as much as six scoops a day. Don't give them too much—that makes them sick. And don't give them too little, or they'll wake us up howling in the middle of the night."

"Hold it," Brenna says. "You're going way too fast. I'll never remember this. Don't you have notes or something?"

"I never use notes. I just remember it."

"You do this every day. This is my first time. Just write it down."

"Do you want a report, too?" I ask as I slam the cupboard shut.

Brenna puts her hands on her hips. "Time-out!" she calls. "What's going on?"

"Everything! Gran has banned me from the clinic until my grades come up. I live here, but I can't work here. I have to write a stupid report or I'll flunk social studies. What's worse, there's

a guy running a puppy mill around here somewhere. Who knows how many puppies need to
be rescued. And oh yeah, I almost forgot, my
starstruck cousin from New York is coming to
stay with us for a while. Gran is expecting me to
wait on her hand and foot. Yippee."

"Wow. That's a lot." She sits cross-legged on
the floor. "The report is the easiest thing to fix.
Work hard and you'll get a good grade. Then Dr.
Mac will let you back in the clinic."

"You don't get it. Even when I work hard, I
get Ds and Fs." I can feel my face turning red.
"School is what I have to sit through until I can
come back home. I could study twenty-four
hours a day and I would still fail. I am not a good
student. I know it. My teachers know it. I wish
Gran would just accept it and leave me alone."

We both stare at the same spot on the floor
for a minute.

"I'm sorry," I say. "It's not your fault. Here." I
grab a piece of paper and quickly jot down some
numbers. "This is what you need to feed the
boarders."

Before Brenna can say anything, David and
Sunita walk in with Gran close behind. She has a
"to do" list for each of them. David has to scrub

the boarding kennels, and Sunita can watch Gran operate the autoclave, the machine that sterilizes Gran's instruments.

"All right. Let's get to work, everybody," Gran says. "Maggie—in the house."

From the look in her eye, I know better than to argue. I turn and leave without saying a word.

Banished, that's what I am.

• • • • • • •

I set up my homework at the kitchen table, and then spend the next two hours doing everything but homework. I turn on ESPN, but there's a golf tournament on. Boring. I try to play ball with Sherlock. He falls asleep. I stretch out on the couch and try to sleep, but thoughts of all the sick pups in the clinic and the puppy mill keep my eyes wide open.

Finally, just as I'm ready to settle down and study, the front doorbell rings. I open it and find a girl with long blond hair standing on the doorstep and a taxi pulling out of the driveway.

"Hi, Maggie! It's me, Zoe!"

Chapter Ten

· · · · · · · · · · · ·

Gran heats up some frozen lasagna and opens a can of corn for dinner—a normal meal for us. Zoe starts to make a face when she sees what's on her plate, but then she claims that lasagna is her favorite food. I can tell she hates it. She eats the corn one kernel at a time and mashes the lasagna into paste while she fills Gran in on her "wonderful" life in New York City.

"I went to a private school that has the worst uniforms on the planet, but I did get to go on good field trips. We went skiing once. In Switzerland."

I look across the table at Gran. Who ever heard

of a school taking kids to Switzerland? Gran shakes her head slightly to signal me to keep quiet.

"What I really like to do is to visit Mom when she's filming at the television studio," Zoe continues. "Everybody on the set knows me and says hi to me. You wouldn't believe how many autographs I have!"

"Do you have a pet?" I ask.

"We lived in a penthouse where pets weren't allowed. Animals are cute to look at, but they're kind of messy. Do you have any sparkling water?"

I get up and pour a glass of water from the tap. "Sorry, this is it."

She puts it down without taking a sip. "Mom says there are more kinds of sparkling water in Los Angeles than you can count. I can't wait to get out there."

"Your mom sounded excited about the new job," Gran says.

Zoe drops her fork and lays her hand on her cheek. "I know! Isn't it amazing?" she says, eyes wide. "She's been waiting for this break for years. A sitcom is just one step away from a major movie deal, you know."

I nod as if I really understand what she's saying. Zoe hasn't changed much since the last time I saw her. She's bubbly, perky, and too dramatic. Her clothes look like they came off a magazine cover. Her hair has a little of the MacKenzie red in it, but it's a lot lighter than mine. She thinks animals are messy. She does not have one single freckle. How can we be related?

Gran lets Zoe talk on and on and on and on until I think I'm hearing bees buzzing. I clear the table and excuse myself. "Homework," I say, taking the stairs two at a time.

Later, when Gran shows Zoe to the bedroom next to mine, I press my ear against the wall to hear what they are saying. Gran is laughing, but I can't make out the words. When was the last time Gran laughed with me?

I bet Zoe gets straight As.

If Gran is going to be so busy with Zoe, then this is a great time to sneak into the clinic and check the pups. I tiptoe down without a sound.

• • • • • • •

Shelby and Inky are fast asleep in their pen. The collies' tummies are rounder, and it seems like they all have normal temperatures. But poor little Dinky is back on an I.V. drip. I read his chart. He still isn't eating or drinking.

I can hear Mitzy barking in her kennel. I wonder if Brenna took her for a walk. She has lots of energy and needs exercise.

One of the collies wakes up and licks my hand. "You want me to stay with you?" I ask him. He gives me a big yawn and blinks his eyes. I think he's the pup who had diarrhea all over Sunita. "You need a name, little guy. What should it be? Oops? No, that's no good. Lucky? No way."

The pup makes a little noise and a big smell.

"Whew! That stinks! I know what to call you—Beans. You know, 'Beans, beans, the musical fruit . . . '" David will get it, even if Gran doesn't.

Beans nibbles on my thumb. I am falling in love. Who could harm such a cute, innocent thing? It makes me so angry that this guy is out there making money off these helpless pups. I've got to track him down, with or without Gran's help.

Gran and Zoe walk in. Uh-oh. I'm caught. Gran raises an eyebrow, but doesn't yell at me.

We are both on our best behavior in front of our guest.

"It's adorable!" squeals Zoe in a high-pitched voice guaranteed to make dogs howl. She runs over to Beans, picks him up without supporting his bottom, and lays him over her shoulder. Before Gran or I can say anything, Beans has another accident all over her very fashionable lime green shirt.

"Ewwww! Gross!" Zoe shrieks.

I can't help myself. I burst out laughing.

Zoe dumps Beans in the pen and runs out of the room with Gran right behind her.

I check the puppy to make sure he isn't hurt. He has this puzzled look in his eyes, as if he's wondering what he did to deserve that kind of treatment.

"It wasn't your fault," I tell him. "She should know better. Pick up a puppy, a sick puppy, and you never know what's going to happen."

A few minutes later, Gran comes in as I'm cleaning up the mess.

"Are you sure we're related to her?" I ask.

"Get upstairs and finish your homework," Gran snaps. "It wasn't nice of you to stand there and laugh at her. She has a lot to get used to."

"But the look on her face was funny."

"I'm very disappointed in you. Go to your room."

I don't get it. Usually Gran has no patience with people who turn up their noses at a little puppy poop. But now she has no patience with me.

I slam the door that divides the kitchen from the clinic and storm back up the steps.

Sherlock wakes up from a nap when I slam the door to my room and flop on my bed. He jumps onto the bed and waddles toward me.

"Go away," I grumble, pushing him to the other side of the bed.

He climbs onto my pillow and licks my face.

"Stop it! You have bad breath!"

Sherlock understands me. He always knows how to get me out of a bad mood.

He sits up and turns his baggy eyes toward my desk where my books are piled up.

"You're right," I say. "Start the extra-credit report."

I drag myself into my chair and open my notebook. Let's see, I have to explain how laws are made in my report. Ms. Griffith told me to connect it to a topic that interests me. So I try to find a way to sneak in information about basketball, but it's hopeless. As far as I can tell, the Pennsylvania state legislature hasn't passed any laws about hoops.

I look at the clock. Gran is still down in the clinic. She's been down there over an hour. Something must be wrong.

"I'm not supposed to go down there," I tell Sherlock. He lifts his head off my pillow. "But I don't think that applies if there's an emergency. Let's go and see if Gran needs help."

Chapter Eleven

• • • • • • • • • • •

Gran has Mitzy, the airhead Airedale, stretched out on the table in the operating room. She whimpers as Gran gently prods her stomach.

"What's wrong?" I ask.

"I'm not sure yet. She was acting antsy, couldn't settle down or stop barking." Gran listens to Mitzy's stomach with her stethoscope and feels her abdomen with her hands. "She's got some air in her stomach, and probably lots of food. How much did you tell Brenna to feed her?"

"Exactly what we always feed her. I even wrote

it down. You don't think the puppies brought in an infection and Mitzy got it, do you?"

"Is it dangerous?"

Gran and I turn around. Zoe is standing by the door. She has changed into a black sweatshirt.

"Mitzy here has a bellyache," Gran says.

"It might be bloat," I say.

"Could be, but she's not in that much pain," says Gran. "Bloat is when a dog gets too much food and air in its stomach. Sometimes the stomach twists, and it can be very dangerous," she explains to Zoe. "That's why I want to keep an eye on her. Maggie, help me get her down. We'll put her in the recovery room. I'll take an X-ray if it gets any worse."

Zoe follows us to the recovery room. She kneels by the puppy pen as we struggle with Mitzy. Now, of course, Mitzy wants to sit. She doesn't want to go into the cage.

"Let me try something," I say. "Mitzy, lie down."

"Don't be silly, Maggie. We don't want her to lie down," Gran says. "We want her in the cage."

"It worked yesterday. She gets things mixed up. Mitzy, come on, honey, lie down!"

Mitzy gives me a mournful look, then steps into the cage. Gran fusses over her, getting her settled in comfortably. I sneak a look at Zoe. She's leaning over the puppy pen. She's not picking up any of the puppies, but she's petting them gently.

I stay with Mitzy for a minute, stroking her nose. "Don't worry, Dr. Gran will help. You'll feel better in the morning, just hang in there." Mitzy thumps her tail once.

Suddenly Zoe gasps and makes a funny noise in her throat. I ignore her. Gran shouldn't let her in the clinic if she's going to keep freaking out about little things. I rub behind Mitzy's ears. "Instead of teaching you how to sit, maybe we'll just go for a short walk tomorrow. Does that sound good?"

Zoe gasps again. Gran looks up from the notes she's writing. "Zoe?"

I turn around. Zoe bites her lip. I scramble over to the puppy pen. Zoe points to Dinky.

"It—it's not breathing," she says. Dinky is very, very still.

Gran is next to us in a flash. She quickly checks Dinky for signs of breathing and a heartbeat.

"Anything?" I ask.

She shakes her head.

"He's gone, Maggie."

• • • • • • •

Bounce. Bounce. Swish.

Bounce. Bounce. Swish.

Shooting baskets in the driveway always helps me feel better, even when it's late at night. Especially when it's late at night.

Bounce. Bounce. Thunk. The ball clangs off the rim and rolls into the shadows. Darn. Now I won't find it until the morning.

"You didn't bend your knees enough," Gran says as she steps out of the darkness holding the ball. "Watch." She dribbles once, bends her knees deeply, and shoots. The ball bounces off the top of the backboard and lands at my feet. No basket.

"You pushed it," I say. "Use your wrist and follow through." I pass the ball to her. "Try again."

She dribbles twice and arcs the ball perfectly into the net.

"Not bad," I joke. "For a grandmother."

"Let's see you do it."

I grab the ball and back up until I'm at the three-point line. I shoot. Air ball. It doesn't even get near the net.

"I'm going in," I say. "I can't do anything right."

"Stay," Gran says. "I think we need to talk."

"About what?" I pick up the ball.

"It's been a rough couple of days."

I shoot from right under the basket. The ball goes in. "It's been a horrible couple of days."

"I'm sorry Dinky died. He was the sickest of all the pups."

"Yeah, I know."

"You're angry at me because I'm letting the other kids volunteer."

I don't answer. Instead I make a layup.

"You're angry at me because you're grounded."

I dribble behind my back and make a jump shot.

"I bet you're angry about Zoe, too."

I shoot too hard and the ball bounces over to Gran. She holds it. "Talk to me, Maggie."

"It feels like I don't live here anymore," I say with a sigh. "There are all these—these people everywhere, and you're mad about school, and my teacher thinks I'm not trying when I really am. It's been so busy, we haven't been able to talk, and I'm really, really upset about the puppies. Can't we just forget that test? I'll do better on the next one, I promise. Tell the kids you don't need them, give Zoe a ticket to L.A., and help me find the puppy mill." I try to steal the ball from her, but she holds on tight.

We stand for a second, both of us clutching the ball. Then Gran lets go.

"You're right," she says. "It's been such a zoo around here I haven't had a chance to think about what all this means to you. Tell you what. We'll keep the kids around until the puppies are healthy and your extra-credit report is done."

"But—" I begin. Gran raises a finger.

"But nothing. You have to do the report. The faster you do it, the faster you're back in the clinic. Maybe one of the kids could help you. They're all pretty nice."

"Ummm."

"OK, Maggie. Once the report is in and the puppies recover, the other kids go home. Happy?"

"What about Zoe?"

Gran's jaw tightens. "Rose and I talked this evening. We decided it would be best for her to stay until school gets out."

"But that's nearly three months! I thought it would be, like, three weeks."

"So did Zoe. But she's putting a good face on it." Gran smiles. "She says maybe she'll train one of our animals to be a movie star."

"Yeah, right."

"She seems determined. Reminds me of you in that way."

I dribble back out to the three-point line. "OK. I do the report and the clinic goes back to normal. I'll be nice to Zoe, and she'll go away, in a while. What about the puppy mill?"

"I'll call the sheriff and give him the information we have, but I doubt it will be high on his list."

"We'll find the creep. I know it," I say, then turn toward the basket. "She shoots!" I release the ball and it swishes through the net. Perfect. "She scores!"

Chapter Twelve

· · · · · · · · · · · ·

The next morning I wake up feeling better. By the time I get dressed, I have a plan. I know how I'm going to find the puppy mill. The trick is to get Gran to the farmer's market.

When I go downstairs, Zoe is already in the kitchen looking in the pantry.

"Don't you guys eat around here?" she asks. "You don't even have any flour. If you had flour, we could make pancakes. Ethel taught me how. Of course, you don't have any maple syrup, but we could have put jam on them . . ." She stands lost in thought, looking at a box of Cheerios. I take the box and pour myself a bowl.

"Gran isn't much of a cook. I can't remember her ever making pancakes. We eat a lot of take-out." That doesn't sound good. "We'll probably go to the store today."

Zoe puts a piece of bread in the toaster and opens the spice cabinet. *Be nice*, I tell myself. *Make conversation.*

"Who is Ethel?" I ask.

She taps her fingernail on the counter. "Our housekeeper."

"Your cleaning lady taught you how to cook?"

"She wasn't a cleaning lady, she was a house-keeper. She ran the house—cooked for us, made sure mom got up in time to get to the studio, helped me with my homework. Ethel was the best."

"Is she in L.A. with your mother?"

"No. Ethel moved back to New Hampshire to take care of her sick brother." Zoe takes a plastic jar of cinnamon out of the cupboard and looks at the date on the bottom. "This is almost as old as I am! Ugh!" She tosses it into the garbage with a shiver. "Do you ever order in breakfast?"

"Did somebody say breakfast?" Gran asks, coming into the kitchen from the clinic.

"Not unless you call toast 'breakfast,'" Zoe says as she wrinkles her nose. "Something's burning."

I leap across the kitchen and pop up the toast.

"Sorry," I say. "I forgot to tell you about the toaster. You have to watch it every second or it turns your toast into charcoal." I lift the charred bread out with my fingertips. "Like this."

"I'll make you a piece," Gran says. "Just let me wash my hands first." She rolls up her sleeves and turns on the faucet, then squirts liquid soap on her hands and scrubs so hard that lather drips into the sink.

"How are Mitzy and the puppies?" I ask Gran.

"Everybody came through the night safely. Mitzy's stomachache is gone, but I want her to have very small meals today." Gran rinses the soap off her hands and dries them on a hand towel decorated with bloodhounds.

"I autopsied Dinky," she says in a quieter voice. "I examined his body to figure out why he died. He was dehydrated and sick with a respiratory infection, but that didn't kill him. Dinky had a congenital heart defect. His heart wasn't formed properly, and it wasn't pumping his blood the right way. Combined with malnourishment and dehydration, he didn't have much of a chance." She tosses the towel at me. "It wasn't anybody's fault."

Except for the guy who mistreated Dinky. The poor pup was so weak, he couldn't hang on any longer. And he had just found a good home. I've got to find a way to get to the farmer's market.

Gran puts more bread in the toaster and bangs down the lever. "I'm sorry there isn't more to choose from," she says to Zoe. "I guess we've been a little busy."

"You need to hire a cook," Zoe says. "Or a housekeeper who will make dinner, at the very least."

"A cook?" Gran asks.

"You should think about it. Everyone I know has one," Zoe says as she plucks her lightly browned toast out of the toaster.

Gran opens the milk carton to pour some milk into her coffee. Three drops come out. "No cooks around here," she says. "And nobody to do the shopping, either."

Now's my chance. I swallow my cereal quickly. "Can we go to the farmer's market?" I ask. "I bet

Zoe's never seen anything like it."

"Good idea," Gran answers. "Gabe has clinic duty, so I can take a few hours off."

Yes!

While Gran shows Zoe how to load the dishwasher—she's never done that before—I sneak off to the clinic. I want to check in on the pups.

They're all sleeping.

"Morning, everybody," I whisper. One of the collies pricks up its ears and rustles a bit. Is there anything cuter than sleeping puppies?

"I'm off to find the creep who treated you so badly. Then we can rescue the other pups—maybe even your brothers and sisters."

• • • • • • •

The market is crowded. There are hundreds of stalls selling a little bit of everything. Gran, Zoe, and I start down one long aisle, past a baker's counter with fresh cinnamon rolls and blueberry muffins, past an Amish farmer and his family selling giant jars of pickled beets, relish, and apple butter. My stomach rumbles.

"How about some hot chocolate?" Gran suggests. "It's not good to shop on an empty stomach."

"That sounds great," Zoe says.

"Maggie?"

"No, thanks. You guys go ahead. I want to look around awhile."

"Are you sure?" Gran asks. "You've never turned down hot chocolate before."

"I'm sure. Go ahead. I'll meet you at the van later."

The two of them walk away without me. Zoe starts chattering a mile a minute, and Gran has a strange smile on her face. It almost seems as if she likes Zoe.

I shake my head. Get a grip. I have more important things to worry about—I'm on a mission.

I start moving down the aisles, asking the farmers if they know of a man who sold puppies at the market last week. It takes a few tries, but Mrs. Nestor, the lady who sells hand-crocheted doll clothes, remembers him.

"Can't recall his name, Maggie." She scratches her head with her crochet hook. "I seen him a few times, here and out in Sayerville. Bent over, scrawny man. Tried to sell me a puppy. I told him, 'What do I need with another dog?'" She laughs and shakes her head. "Cute pups, but they were just as skinny as he was."

This has to be the same guy. "Can you remember anything about him? What kind of car he drove, if he had anybody working with him, stuff like that?"

"Nope, nothing." She pulls a ball of purple yarn out of the bag at her feet. "He lives on Lafayette Road. Did tell me that. Does that help you any?"

"That's great! Oh my gosh, Mrs. Nestor, you've helped a lot! Thank you, thank you so much." I'd like to give her a hug, but that is a very large crochet hook she's holding.

"Think nothing of it. Glad I could help, Maggie. Give my best to your grandmother."

"Thanks again," I call as I jog down the aisle. I am going to get this guy. We'll close him down. Just wait until I find Gran. She'll be pumped, too. This puppy mill is history.

• • • • • • •

I find Gran and Zoe standing by the popcorn stand. As Gran pays for a bag of popcorn, Zoe says something and the popcorn vendor laughs. Gran puts her arm around Zoe's shoulder and gives it a squeeze. Zoe tosses some popcorn at Gran.

That was dumb. No way Gran is going to stand for that.

But Gran laughs and shakes her head as she picks the popcorn out of her hair. If I had done that, I bet she'd lecture me. But she doesn't lecture Zoe. Instead she steals a handful of popcorn out of Zoe's bag and tries to shove it in her mouth. Zoe squeals and everybody laughs again. This is sickening.

They leave the popcorn vendor and walk straight toward me.

"Oh, there you are, Maggie," Gran says.

"Yeah," I answer.

"Did you find what you were looking for?"

She doesn't want to hear about the puppy mill owner. She's having too much fun with Zoe. And I don't really want to tell her, not in front of Zoe.

Gran studies my face. "Is something wrong?"

"No, everything's fine," I say, trying to smile. "I'm ready to go."

Chapter Thirteen

• • • • • • • • • • •

Gran planned out the rest of the weekend for me. I had to do "everything in my power" to help Zoe settle in. That meant clearing some of my stuff from the guest room. I have a lot of stuff. Old soccer uniforms, a dozen pairs of sneakers that don't fit me but are too important to throw away, tests I never got around to showing Gran ... and that was just one layer of junk in the closet.

Once the guest room was sort of clean, Gran made me sit down to finish correcting my social studies test. I even had to fix my spelling mistakes. That took forever.

Now it's Monday morning—back to school.

Before Zoe and I leave for the bus stop, I say good-bye to Mitzy. Her owners are coming to pick her up today.

"Make sure Gran tells them that 'Lie down!' means 'Come,'" I tell Mitzy. She licks my face, a very polite doggy good-bye. I'll miss her mixed-up ways. Strange but true.

When I get on the bus, I find an empty seat so Zoe and I can sit together. But she takes a seat next to Caitlin Samboro. And by the time we get to Elizabeth Blackwell Elementary, Zoe and Caitlin are acting like best friends. And Gran told me to watch out for her today, this being her first day at a new school and all. Go figure.

• • • • • • •

My class has library on Monday. I usually hate it, but today I'm grateful for the quiet. It gives me a chance to think and plan. I find a table by the window and make a list of what I know about the puppy mill so far.

litter of sick collies sold at the
    farmer's market
black labs, too

and the mutt
the guy lives on Lafayet Road

I chew on my eraser. I don't know much.
What should I do next? I doubt they have a book
that lists people who don't take good care of
their pets. I suppose I could ask a librarian, but I
hate asking for help—it makes me feel stupid.

I look around. Everyone is actually doing
homework. I see Sunita sitting on the floor, her
feet tucked neatly under her legs. Gran told me
to think about asking the kids for help. Sunita is
the smartest of them, no question. And she's the
sweetest. I bet she won't make me feel stupid.
Here goes.

I walk over and explain my problem.

"Wait, I'm confused," Sunita says. "What are
you going to do when you find this man?"

"I don't know," I admit. "I haven't thought
that far ahead."

She closes her book and stands up. "There
have been some laws about animal abuse passed
recently. That's where we should start. Come
on." She heads for the reference desk.

"Do we have to ask a librarian?"

"Yes. We'll find what we need faster if Mr.

Margate helps us." She smiles at Mr. Margate and explains what she's looking for. He pulls out a giant book from the shelf by his desk. "You want information about the puppy mill law," he says. "It'll be in here. This book contains all the laws of the Commonwealth of Pennsylvania."

We carry the book to my table, and I open to the table of contents. The words look like millions of ants marching down the page. All I can do is stare.

"What's wrong?" Sunita asks.

I look at her. I have to ask her to help me read. If I don't, I'll never be able to help shut down that puppy mill.

"Um, I, it's just that, well... I don't read so good. It takes me forever and then I forget what I just read." I can feel sweat on my forehead, and my stomach is ready to bolt for the door. If she laughs at me I think I'll die.

"Oh, that's not a problem. I'll help."

That's it? That's all she's going to say? I wish Gran would take that attitude.

Sunita scans the table of contents, flips to the index, then dives in. It's like watching a great author or something the way she reads so fast and scribbles notes.

"Voilà! The Dog Purchaser Protection Act, Section 9.3. OK. Here's the deal. People who raise puppies for sale are required to provide them with a healthy environment."

"Well, he didn't do that."

"They also have to be honest about any diseases the puppies might have."

"He lied. Strike two."

"They have to make sure the pups are given the proper vaccinations, and they aren't allowed to treat them badly."

"We've got him! This guy really is breaking the law. Excellent! What can we do to him?"

"A couple of years ago, it was totally legal to mistreat puppies. Now anyone who breaks this new law has to pay big fines. He could even be sent to jail."

"That's so great!"

"Shhh!" Mr. Margate hisses from across the room.

"That's so great," I whisper. "We can shut him down."

"What do we do next?" Sunita asks. She's just as excited as I am.

"Hang on. I better write this down so I don't forget it. This is important."

The Dog Purchaser Protection Act
Section 9.3

Breeders have to provide...	If not...
a good place to live	~~fins~~ fines
~~vackcinashun~~ vacinacion	JAIL!
health records	

"You spelled some words wrong," Sunita says.

"I don't care. What mattters is that we can put this guy in jail!"

"Or at the very least, put him out of the dog breeding business," says Sunita. "But we have to find him first. Guess where we have to look."

"I know," I say. "Back to the librarian's desk." Twice in one day. I wonder if I'm going to have an allergic reaction.

Mr. Margate takes back the law book and shows us where we can find a special phone directory that lists people by address. After Sunita corrects my spelling of the street name, we find the listings for Lafayette Road. They take up three pages. If I have to call everyone on this road, it will take forever.

I need help.

"What are you doing after school?" I ask Sunita.

* * * * * * *

The bus ride home is loud and bumpy as usual. What's different is that Sunita is sitting next to me instead of her usual seat behind the driver. She has to shout so I can hear her.

"Even with both of us it could take days!" she hollers.

"What do you mean?"

She opens her binder to a page of calculations. "I did the math. Fifty names per column, three columns per page, three pages of columns equals four hundred and fifty names. Even if each phone call takes three minutes, it will take the two of us more than eleven hours!"

"You're joking."

She shakes her head.

"What if Brenna helps us?"

She slides her calculator out of a special pocket in her binder. How does she keep a notebook that neat?

"Seven point five hours."

"And if we add Zoe?"

"About five and a half."

That would still take two afternoons of calling. Gran wouldn't let four of us stay on the phone from 3:30 until 9:00 P.M. I look at the back of the bus. David is making faces with his buddies, turning up his nose and crossing his eyes. I can't believe I'm going to do this.

"And David?"

"If there are five of us, taking ninety names each, three minutes a name, it comes down to four and a half hours. That's less than half of what it would take if there were two of us. Oh, and if you do it alone"—she pauses for a quick calculation—"it will take twenty-two point five hours."

I have to take back what I said to my teacher about math being useless.

Each time the bus stops, I scoot down the aisle to talk to one of the others. Brenna is drawing a peace symbol on the back of her left hand with a green marker. She agrees instantly. Zoe is two rows back sitting with the Conover twins, who are the coolest kids in fifth grade. When I ask her if she'll help, she smiles and says, "Sure.

Mom always said I was good at talking on the phone."

As I step to the back row, the boys freeze. I still can't believe I'm doing this.

"David, do you want to come to the clinic? We need your help."

His friends erupt into screams, hoots, and hollers. He blushes, which makes matters worse. I turn to walk away. This was a stupid idea.

David yells loud enough to be heard over the noise.

"I'll be there!"

I stumble back to my seat and sit back down next to Sunita. "Remind me again why we're doing this," I mutter.

The bus lets us off at the corner. We troop into the clinic, me at the head of the pack and Zoe bringing up the rear. Dr. Gabe is searching through the piles of paper on the receptionist's desk.

"Hi, Gabe. Where's Gran?"

"She's out on a call to Mr. Barber's," he explains. "Hoof rot. Again."

"Mr. Barber will talk forever," I say. "We have all the time we need."

Sunita hands out the photocopied phone lists, and I assign people to the telephones. David gets the house line in the kitchen, Zoe takes the phone in Gran's bedroom, and Sunita calls from the phone in the lab. Before she starts, she disconnects the modem and attaches it to an old phone, so Brenna and I each have a phone to use at the receptionist's desk. And there is still one phone line open for incoming calls. Having six telephone lines is another advantage of living next to the clinic.

"OK, guys, listen up," I say as we gather around the kitchen table. "This is really important. If we can find the puppy mill, then we can rescue the rest of the dogs and shut this guy down for good. But first we have to find out where they are. Don't rush, and make sure you call every number."

"What do we say?" Sunita asks. "I'm not a very good liar."

"You don't have to lie. Just ask if they have puppies for sale. Say you got the number from a friend."

"Which is the truth," Brenna points out.

"Those puppies are counting on us. Start dialing!"

We get to work. Dial, ask, and hang up. Dial, ask, and hang up. Brenna is great at this. Her voice sounds so confident. I'm having trouble. I keep getting wrong numbers. I always get wrong numbers.

Brenna hangs up her phone and watches me dial. After a minute she says, "You're not dialing the numbers on your sheet. You're switching them. Instead of 463-9257, you just dialed 436-2597."

"Darn. That happens a lot...Wait. That means—oh, my gosh! I know what happened to Mitzy!"

"What are you talking about?" Brenna asks.

"Where's that piece of paper I gave you, the one with the feeding instructions?"

"Taped to the cupboard back in the kennel. Why?"

No time to explain. I sprint to the kennel and find the chart. I take a deep breath and carefully read what I wrote.

Yep, I was right. I switched the numbers. Brenna fed Mitzy exactly what I wrote down, but I wrote down 5.2 scoops of dry food a day instead of 2.5 scoops a day. We're lucky it wasn't more serious.

I lean against the wall. Mitzy got hurt because of my mistake. I put a patient in danger—

"Maggie, Maggie!" Sunita shouts. "David found the puppy seller!"

Chapter Fourteen

. . . .

It only took a few minutes to explain what we found to Gran, but it took a couple of days for her to pull together "the necessary arrangements." At first, I didn't want to wait, but then I could sort of see her point. She wanted to do things properly so the animals would be taken care of and the authorities would go along with us.

But Brenna grumbled about it all week. She thought we should just swoop in and rescue the pups. Sneak in at night and steal them if we had to. Even I could see that was a bad idea. David and Zoe cooked up a scheme to notify the television stations so we could be on the news, but Gran put an end to that one.

Finally the big day is here. As we drive through the pouring rain out to Lafayette Road, Gran goes over what we might see one more time.

"Good breeders raise animals properly. They provide them with clean cages and plenty of food and water. They vaccinate them, and they are careful to breed only animals who are strong and healthy, and have good personalities.

"You won't see any of that where we're going. Chances are it's going to be filthy. The dogs will be underfed and sick. The people who run these places don't care about the health or happiness of the animals. They just want to make money fast."

"Sounds scary," says Zoe.

"You can stay in the van if you want," Gran offers. "There's nothing wrong with making that choice."

I look back at the others. David is anxious, Brenna outraged, Sunita worried, Zoe concerned. No one is backing out. We're going to see this through to the end.

We pull in a gravel driveway and drive past a hand-painted sign that says PUPPIES 4 SALE.

The animal shelter van and a sheriff's car pull in behind us. They are here to help us. Captain Thompson heads up the local shelter. He retired from the army a few years ago. His full name is Zebulon P. Thompson. Whenever I ask him what the *P* stands for, he always has a different answer. I mostly call him "sir."

His volunteers will take any healthy animals we find to the shelter. Then they'll try to find good homes for them. The sheriff is here to make sure that everything is done legally.

We park next to a two-story farmhouse. In front of us is a small barn missing some windows and desperate for a coat of paint. A wet cat darts past the van and hides under the front porch. I can hear a bunch of dogs barking. They are not happy barks. They are pained, sad barks.

A man runs out of the house without a coat on. He must be the owner. Mrs. Nestor was right—he is skinny. Mean-tempered, too.

"What do you people think you're doing?" he screams as he bangs on my side of the van. "Get off my property. I don't want you here!"

"Do you think he has a gun?" Sunita whispers.

"I don't care," says Brenna boldly.

"I care," David says. "I care a lot."

"David's right," says Gran as she turns off the engine. "You should care. Wait here, kids, until I make sure it's safe for you to get out."

The sheriff and Gran talk briefly, then she knocks on my window.

"You can come out if you want."

The puppy mill owner shakes his finger in the sheriff's face as we all get out of the van.

"Sheriff, I want these people arrested right now," he demands, shaking with anger.

The sheriff crosses his arms over his chest. Rain drips from the front of his hat and makes a puddle at his feet. "They made me get a warrent, Larry. It's about your dogs. Bunch of people filed complaints. We need to take a look at them now. If they're in bad shape, the doc here can take them away."

Larry, the puppy mill owner, looks behind him, toward the sound of barking, howling dogs. "I haven't had a chance to clean 'em up today. The rain and all, you know," he says. "Come back tomorrow."

The sheriff looks at Gran. "It would be nicer to do this in better weather," he comments.

"Then he'll fix everything up," I interrupt.

"That's not fair. We—I mean Gran—has to inspect the dogs now!"

"She's right," Gran says.

"I'm calling my lawyer!" Larry yells. He turns around and stomps toward the house.

"Let's get this over with," says the sheriff.

Captain Thompson and his volunteers walk toward the front of the barn. Gran heads the other way, around the back of it. Brenna and I follow Gran. Sunita, David, and Zoe follow Captain Thompson.

From the sound of the barking, I figure there will be four dogs, maybe five, plus a few puppies. I am completely unprepared for what we see as we turn the corner.

It looks like a jail, a horrible jail for dogs. Dogs are crammed into small wire kennels, two rows of them. I count ten kennels per row. Brenna and I walk down the middle of the aisle, speechless. This guy has been breeding chocolate and yellow Labs, collies, and a few terriers. There are so many animals that look hungry and dirty, I don't know where we should start.

The kennels are awful. There is nothing protecting the animals from the rain. The dogs are crowded into the wire cages and have to go to the bathroom right where they sit. The stench is horrifying. Their food bowls are disgusting. I see worms everywhere. A scrawny Lab is struggling to lap up water from a puddle.

A few dogs bark wildly at us. The rest look too malnourished to make any noise. Some have open sores where their fur has been rubbed away, probably from rubbing up against the cages, trying to get out.

I blink fast to get rid of the tears in my eyes. How could anyone treat animals this way?

"I wonder how he'd feel if we locked him up in a cage," Brenna growls.

"He doesn't have feelings," Gran mutters.

David runs around the corner of the barn. "We found puppies in the barn!" Sunita and Zoe follow, each cradling a terrier puppy in her jacket.

"Oh, my gosh." Zoe is stunned at the sight of the kennels.

"Are those . . . ?" begins Sunita. She covers her mouth with her hand.

David can't say anything. He's speechless.

"The owner must keep puppies in the barn for a few days to clean them up and put some weight on them before he sells them," Gran says.

"Let's get them out of here," I say. "Let's get them home."

It takes more than an hour for Captain Thompson's volunteers to remove the dogs from the kennels. Gran does a quick examination and decides who is healthy enough to go to the shelter, and who needs to go to the clinic. They are all hungry. As the volunteers load up the shelter van, Gran tells Captain Thompson how to feed them properly. The shelter van has to make two trips.

When Gran is ready to take the sick dogs and puppies back to the clinic, she starts up the van and turns the heat on full blast.

"Get in out of the rain," she tells us. "You are all going to have to be puppy incubators." We jump in the van and she starts handing each of us three puppies bundled in a towel. "Hold them close. They need your body heat."

Sunita nudges me. I look out the window. The sheriff and the puppy mill owner are shaking hands. They are smiling at each other.

"He looks awfully happy for a guy who was just arrested," remarks Zoe.

"Here, guys, help me," I say. "Hold my puppies for a minute." Brenna, David, and Sunita each take one of my puppies. I open the door and dash out into the storm. Lightning flashes. I count one, two, three, four, five. The thunder rumbles. That was close. I'm petrified, but I keep going.

"Excuse me!" I say to the sheriff as I tap him on the back. "Aren't you going to arrest him?"

He turns to me. "That's not necessary. The doc has the sick animals. Larry here, he tried his best."

"I lost my job," Larry says.

"He lost his job," the sherifff repeats. "Then he hurt his back."

"I couldn't take care of them," Larry says. He shakes his head from side to side, as if he really cared about the dogs. What a fake! What a total fake!

"I gave him a warning, and he promised to help out with your grandmother's vet fees. You should get back in the van."

The thunder booms again.

Now I'm shaking.

I'm furious.

I fumble in my pocket and pull out my notes

from the library. "You have to charge him," I tell the sheriff. I read slowly, "According to The Dog Purchaser Protection Act, Section 9.3, an amendment to the Unfair Trade Practices and Consumer Protection Law. He didn't give customers a health record or a health certificate signed by a vet. Plus he isn't taking care of the dogs out back. Half of them look . . ." My throat closes up.

Don't cry, I tell myself. *Don't cry yet. Use the facts.* I stare Larry the Liar straight in the eye.

"Half of them look like they're ready to die. You should be charged with neglect, abuse, and cruelty." I hand my notes to the sheriff.

"Hang on," says the sheriff. He uses his radio to contact his office and explain the situation. We wait a very long minute—the sheriff tapping his boot impatiently, me glaring at Larry, Larry trying to figure out if he should look sad, angry, or embarrassed.

The radio crackles, and the sheriff listens closely to his dispatcher. Then he looks up.

"The kid is right, Larry. I don't have a choice. I have to charge you. Get in the car. We'll do this down at the station."

Yes!

I turn around. Gran is standing behind me.

She must have been standing there the whole time in case something went wrong, but she let me do it on my own. Her hair is plastered to her head, and the rain has soaked her sweatshirt, but her eyes are warm and proud.

"You did it!" she shouts over the thunder. She gives me quick hug. "That's my girl!"

I haven't heard her say that in a really, really long time.

Chapter Fifteen

• • • • • • • • • • •

The clinic looks like a veterinarian's version of *101 Dalmatians*. Dogs, dogs, dogs everywhere, big and small, and they all need a doctor. Thank goodness we have enough of those. Dr. Gabe put out the call for help while we were at the puppy mill. A couple of his friends from vet school are here to pitch in.

Gran directs traffic. "I want each dog to have a number, an ID tag, and a chart. Gabe, you hand out the numbers. We need to keep them straight. Use both of the exam rooms, the O.R., and the recovery room. If we need extra space, move the lab equipment into the kitchen."

"Excuse me," says a young vet with cornrows. She rushes past the five of us holding a panting terrier. "Where's your X-ray machine?" she asks Gran. "I think this one has a punctured lung."

"Down the hall to your right," Gran says.

We're in the way. David sits in a chair in the waiting room and puts his feet up so no one will trip over them. Zoe heads for the kitchen.

"I guess I should go home," says Sunita. "Can I use your phone?"

"Yeah. Follow Zoe. Hang on, I'll come with you."

I open the door to the kitchen.

"Margaret MacKenzie, where are you going?" Gran shouts across the room.

I turn around.

"I need you in here," Gran says.

My heart starts to beat faster. "You do?"

"Yes! I need all of you. Scrub up and get into the recovery room. We need all the hands and eyes we can get."

While Gran, Gabe, and the visiting vets do the doctor work, Brenna, Sunita, David, Zoe, and I are responsible for everything else. This time we know what we're doing.

David is in charge of transporting stabilized patients back to recovery. He isn't joking around. Instead he's quiet and fast. Sunita and Brenna move Shelby and Inky in with the collie pups and the mutt, then use the empty puppy pen as a nursery. Sunita turns on the heat lamp so her patients won't catch a chill.

"What can I do to help?" Zoe asks.

"Stand by the oxygen cage," Gran says, pointing. "Watch the patients inside. If any of them starts breathing fast, count the number of breaths per minute. If more than fifty, you let me know ASAP—as soon as possible."

I'm in charge of supplies. I drop off packages of clean instruments to each team and stock them with antibiotics and gloves. "We're going to run out of Ringer's solution," I warn Gran.

The veterinarian with cornrows tosses me a set of car keys. "The VW bug outside is mine. You'll find two boxes of supplies on the backseat. I like to come prepared."

"A woman after my own heart," says Gran. "Next!"

I dash out into the rain and come back with the boxes. As I drop off the extra I.V. bags, I

watch David. He's carrying a pair of young terriers on a stretcher and is headed straight for an
instrument cart.

"Look out!"

He's already seen it. He holds the stretcher
steady and eases by the cart. He didn't drop anything. Amazing.

The storm rolls around us, with plenty of
lightning and window-rattling thunder. The
dogs in the boarding kennels are terrified. They
howl and scratch at their cage doors.

"Will somebody please calm those dogs
down," orders Gran.

"I'll do it," says Brenna. "Will you be all right
alone?" she asks Sunita. Sunita nods, and Brenna
jogs down the hall and around the corner.

I do a quick check of the puppies in the pen.
They're all breathing steadily. So far, so good.
There are more fleas here than I have ever seen
at one time, but things are under control.

Lightning strikes nearby. The lights flicker.
The boarding dogs howl and moan again.

"Oh, that's just what we need," says Gabe.
"More excitement."

The lights stay on.

"Don't worry," Gran says. "If the power goes

out, I have an emergency generator. Working by candlelight doesn't appeal to me."

"I don't know," Gabe shouts from the other room. "It could be kind of romantic."

Gran rolls her eyes and laughs. The tension is fading. The recovery-room cages are nearly full. The vets in the exam rooms are cleaning up. It looks like we're almost finished.

Suddenly Gran goes silent. The tiny yellow Lab in her hands is failing fast.

"Help me, Maggie. Get me oxygen."

"One canister is empty, and Dr. Gabe is using the other," I say.

The puppy stops breathing.

"Oh no you don't," Gran says. She bends down and blows into the pup's nose, very gently so she doesn't damage the lungs. After each puff, Gran listens to the heartbeat. Puff, listen, puff, listen.

"Breathe, breathe…" Gran urges the puppy.

I run to the operating room. "Gran is doing artificial respiration on a Lab," I tell Gabe. "She can't do it all night, and you have the last canister of oxygen. What should we do?"

"Time for a little trip," Dr. Gabe tells the puppy on the table. "I'll carry the dog, you bring the canister." He picks up the pup and steadies the oxygen mask on its face. I roll the canister of oxygen close by so the pup in Dr. Gabe's arms can keep using it.

Dr. Gabe sets his puppy down next to Gran's. "OK, fellas, it's time to learn about sharing. My patient's not in distress anymore," he tells Gran. "Let's try alternating the mask between the two of them."

Gran takes the small oxygen mask off Dr. Gabe's puppy and puts it on the one she's helping. I cross my fingers. *Breathe, breathe.* Gran puts her stethoscope on the puppy again. All of a sudden, the little Lab wrinkles her nose and coughs. She takes a deep breath. She's going to make it.

• • • • • • •

It's past eleven o'clock when Gran drives the other kids home. They all left tired but satisfied knowing that they had helped save a lot of animals today. The puppies we rescued—all twenty-five of them—are asleep, but Zoe and I are too keyed up to go to bed.

"Want some hot chocolate?" I ask.

"Sure. But not that kind," she says as I pull the packets of instant hot chocolate mix out of the pantry. "That stufff tastes like chemicals. We'll make it from scratch. Ethel taught me how."

I put the instant away and get out the real cocoa.

"I'm so psyched," Zoe says. "Get out the sugar and the milk. It was just amazing. Well, not the puppy mill—that was disgusting. I thought I was going to vomit. But it was so cool how we went in there and saved all those dogs. Here, give that to me, you're making a mess."

She pours the milk into a pan.

"How can you do that without measuring?" I ask.

"Practice." She turns on the burner and adds the sugar and cocoa. "Here." She hands me a wooden spoon. "Don't stop stirring."

Sherlock trots into the room. He stops in his tracks, stunned by the sight of me cooking at the stove. "Give him a biscuit," I say. "I don't want him having a heart attack or anything."

Zoe reaches into the cookie jar and tosses Sherlock his treat. Now he's really confused. I'm the only one who gives him biscuits. The whole world is upside down tonight.

Zoe joins me at the stove and takes the spoon from me. "If you don't stir it fast enough, you'll scald it. And you don't want it to boil." She turns off the stove. "There, now taste this."

I hate to admit it, but she's right. Hot chocolate from scratch tastes much better. I pour the hot chocolate into two mugs and hand one over to her.

"Is it always like this around here?" she asks.

"It's not usually quite so hectic, but we have our moments."

"It reminded me of an emergency-room scene in my mom's old show. There was an earthquake in the town and all these people kept rushing to the E.R. and my mom was trapped in a collapsed building." She stops to blow on her hot chocolate. "But that was just pretend. This was real."

"Isn't it about time for bed?" Gran asks as she walks in from the clinic.

Zoe yawns. "I'm going to have terrible bags under my eyes in the morning."

"You can sleep in," Gran promises.

"Ciao!" Zoe says with a little wave.

"Good night," Gran and I call.

I wait until Zoe is out of earshot. "Bags under her eyes? Chow?"

"Ciao means good-bye in Italian. Give her a break, Maggie."

"It would be easier if she talked like a normal kid. But she does make good hot chocolate."

Gran pours the rest of the hot chocolate into a mug and sits down across from me.

"All our patients are doing great," she reports.

I grin. "The MacKenzie clan rescues the day."

"You were the one who got the whole ball rolling. You found the puppy mill and made sure the owner was arrested. You have a passion for helping animals, Maggie. You're going to be a great vet someday."

I swish the last of my hot chocolate around in the bottom of my mug. "I'll never be a veterinarian unless my grades come up—especially math. I think you're right, Gran." I swallow what's left. "I need that tutor." I tell her about Mitzy and how I switched the numbers.

She takes a deep breath. "Well, I'm glad you told me. Just remember there's nothing wrong with asking for help now and then. We could never have managed on our own tonight. I couldn't have done it without the other vets, and your friends did a terrific job."

"We're a good team," I agree. "David kept everyone's spirits up, Sunita was like a pool of calmness in the middle of the confusion, and those poor dogs in the boarding kennels would have been terrified without Brenna."

Gran gets up and carries our empty mugs to the sink. "Still, I made you a promise. As soon as things are back to normal, I'll tell them that we don't need their help anymore. I never thought I would say this, but I'm going to miss those kids."

Chapter Sixteen

· · · · · · · · · · · ·

The following Saturday, Gran and Zoe chase me out of the house right after breakfast.

Something is up.

I hop on my bike and ride down to my tutor's. She's a retired teacher named Mrs. Shea who has a house filled with birds and a brain filled with tricks to help kids with their schoolwork. This is my second tutoring session. So far, so good.

"Tell me about the extra-credit report," Mrs. Shea says, once we are settled in her living room.

"Well, I got an A for content. The teacher really

liked my idea of writing about the new puppy mill law, and she said I explained it well. But I got a C for mechanics—I lost points for spelling. The stupid spell checker on my computer missed all kinds of words."

"I told you to use the dictionary."

"Yeah, I know. You were right. It's so unfair."

Mrs. Shea smiles. "Let's get to your homework."

• • • • • • •

When I get home two hours later, Brenna, David, and Sunita are hanging out on the front lawn.

"Hi, guys. What are you all doing out here?" I try the doorknob, but it's locked.

"Dr. Mac won't let us in," David explains.

"What?"

"We all got these this morning," Sunita says, handing me an invitation. It isn't very fancy, and the handwriting looks suspiciously like Gran's.

"OK, you guys, what is this about?"

"We got here a little early, but your grandmother wouldn't let us in," says Brenna. "She said we have to wait until exactly—"

"Twelve noon," announces Sunita, looking at her watch. "That would be now."

The door swings open.

"Welcome!" says Gran with a funny smile on her face.

"Do you feel all right?" I ask her.

No answer. She turns and walks into the kitchen. We follow her.

The kitchen smells like cake. I don't think our kitchen has ever smelled like cake before. Zoe stands by the sink, which is piled high with dirty mixing bowls and cake pans. She wiggles her eyebrows at me. Aha! Now this is beginning to make sense.

"Sit down, sit down," Gran says.

We sit. Zoe sets down a giant cake. It is covered with white frosting and has the words "Thank You" written in the middle of what looks like chocolate icing. Tiny puppies made out of frosting tumble around the base of the cake.

"Anybody want a piece?" she asks.

David and Brenna both shout, while Sunita says, "Yes, please." Zoe hands Gran a knife, and she cuts five fat pieces.

My grandmother is throwing a party? This is too weird.

"This was your cousin's idea," Gran mumbles as she hands me a plate. "She wanted to bring in a caterer, but I drew the line there." Then she straightens up and says louder, "I have good news. Captain Thompson has found homes for nearly all the dogs he took back to the shelter. He came by this morning to take pictures of the puppies that we have left. He's going to start a waiting list for when they are stronger and ready to go to a home."

"A good home," Zoe adds.

I hear a noise and look under the table. The little mutt that almost escaped from me a couple of weeks ago is playing with Sherlock's tail. "He got out again," I announce.

"He has a name," Zoe announces as she picks him up. Her animal handling is improving a bit. "I named him Sneakers. Gran said we might get to keep him."

"What? You never let us keep puppies."

"I know, I know," Gran says as she cuts herself a slice of cake. "But this little one got to me. He kept sneaking over to the house, like he belongs here. One day I found him sleeping in Zoe's bed.

That was the last straw." She winks. "Besides, Zoe needs a pet. More cake?"

"What about the first puppies, the Labs?" asks Sunita. "What happened to them?" She hasn't been here for the last few days because of ballet lessons.

"The lady who brought in Shelby, the first pup, decided to give him to the twins. Inky and Shelby were great buddies. It's nice that they got to go to the same home," I explain. I push my plate back. "I'm stuffed."

Socrates stalks in, waving his tail. He jumps up into Sunita's lap. Gran lifts an eyebrow. Socrates never sits in anyone's lap. I hear a little growl under the table. Sneakers is climbing on top of Sherlock's head. Sherlock gives me a look of dismay, and I sneak him some vanilla frosting. Gran would kill me if she saw that, but it looks like she's getting ready to make a speech. She clears her throat and stands up.

"The purpose of this little party is to thank you all for your hard work," she says. "I don't know what the past few weeks would have been like without your help. So as a token of my appreciation, I have a present for each of you."

She takes a cardboard box from the closet,

sets it on the table, and pulls out an envelope.

"For Brenna, a donation to an animal rescue charity of your choice. Your passion and outrage remind me of somebody I knew a long time ago."

"Wow! Thanks. I'll give it to Captain Thompson," Brenna declares. "For the shelter."

"Sunita, your very own book on feline anatomy." Sunita blushes as she takes the book in her hands. Socrates rubs his cheek on the corner of the book, then closes his eyes in contentment.

"David, a Three Stooges video. Every comedian needs good material. For Zoe, your very own lab coat so you don't ruin any more shirts. And I didn't forget you either, Maggie. A calculator, one that prints out your work on a strip of paper. That way you can check to make sure you entered in the right number."

I can feel myself blushing. "Does it check spelling, too?"

"'Fraid not. Listen up, please."

We all put down our forks. Gran pushes up her sleeves and sticks her hands in her pockets.

"I'm not very good at speeches," she says, "but I do want to say thank you. You surprised me. You were a good team. But now that things are back to normal, I'm afraid that we won't need—"

"Did the delivery truck get here yet?" asks Dr. Gabe, poking his head through the door from the clinic. "Hey, cake! Is there enough for me?"

"There's enough for everybody," I say.

While Gran cuts him a piece, I look around the table. There's Brenna, who would lead a protest march in an instant. David, cracking knock-knock jokes trying to get Sunita to smile. Sunita, fingering the anatomy book and petting Socrates. Across the table, Zoe, my cousin, who could not be more different from me . . . and me. We do make a good team. Too good to split up.

I stand up before I realize what I'm doing. I have something to say.

"Ahem." Nobody notices. "A-hem!"

Everybody stops talking.

"Thank you. I want to say something. Gran, I want to remind you of all the times you've scolded me for not asking for help, for not staying after school, or for not telling you I was stuck."

"You don't have to remind me of that," she says with a smile. "I know all about it."

I take a deep breath.

"I'm learning, slowly, that asking for help is a good thing."

Everybody is quiet now. Even Dr. Gabe has stopped chewing. It's time to jump in with both feet.

"I was a little hurt when you invited Brenna to work here. Then David and Sunita were in, and I was out. And to top it off, Zoe came to stay. I felt like I was losing my place here—like I wasn't needed anymore." I stop.

"Let me try to say this better. There is plenty of work at a veterinary clinic. Jobs that I can do. That we can do. That they"—I point to Brenna, David, Sunita, and Zoe—"can do. I think we should let them stay. If we had their help, you would have more time to write your column and do research. And I would spend more time studying or with my tutor, I promise."

I pause. The only sound is Socrates purring.

"I want us to work together."

Gran's left eyebrow shoots up. I know what she's thinking.

"Yes. I'm sure," I tell her.

Gran takes her plate to the sink, rinses it,

and puts it in the dishwasher. We watch her in silence, our heads turning as she walks to the door of the clinic.

Did I say the wrong thing?

Gran pauses at the door, then turns around.

"Well? What are you waiting for?" she asks. Her eyes light up her face. "Let's get to work!"

Puppy-Proof Your Home

BY J.J. MACKENZIE, D.V.M.

Puppies love to explore. Unfortunately, they do most of it with their mouths. They'll chomp, chew, or slobber on almost anything that catches their eye. So how do you prevent your puppy from swallowing the chicken bones in the garbage or chewing on your soccer cleats?

Clean up. Many household cleaning products are poisonous to your puppy. Move all cleaning products, fertilizers, antifreeze, poisons, and detergents to a high shelf your puppy can't get to.

Put down the lid. Curious puppies can jump or fall into the toilet and drown, so keep the lid down.

Crawl around. Get down on your hands and knees and crawl around to see what the house looks like from your puppy's perspective. Look under the bed, behind the couch, under the dresser. Move electrical cords, hair barrettes, plastic bags, and any small objects that your puppy can swallow.

> **PUPPIES CAN SWALLOW SMALL OBJECTS, LIKE HAIR BARRETTES.**

Keep neat. Pick up newspapers, books, toys, sports equipment, shoes, and dirty clothes. Your puppy thinks they are chew toys.

Check plants. Many houseplants, such as aloe vera and poinsettia, are poisonous to dogs. Outdoor plants can harm them, too. Dogs can get very sick if they chew on plants like azaleas or tomato vines. Also keep your dog away from lawns that have been treated recently with chemicals.

Take out the garbage. The garbage is full of dangerous things that can hurt your puppy, like chicken bones and metal cans. Never leave a dog alone with a garbage can. At best, you'll have a mess to clean up. At worst, you'll have a medical emergency.

Keep her on a leash. Never take your puppy off her leash in an unfenced yard. She could chew poisonous plants, swallow mulch, have a run-in with another animal, or wander into the street.

DOCTOR ON CALL

If your puppy has any of these symptoms, pick up the phone and call your vet. It could be a sign that your puppy is sick.

- Swollen stomach
- Loss of energy
- Excessive coughing, panting, or gasping
- Fainting
- Vomiting, for more than 12 hours
- Diarrhea, for more than a day
- Fever or shivers
- Red eyes
- Smelly, dirty ears
- Worms in stool
- Excessive scratching
- Limping
- Lump or bumps under the skin
- Bleeding
- Inability to go to the bathroom
- Dragging bottom on the ground